555

VOLUME 1:
NONE SO WORTHY

CB555-01: 555 Vol. 1: None So Worthy
ISBN: 978-0-9962768-2-5

Carrion Blue 555
Chicopee MA / Lambertville NJ
carrionblue555@gmail.com

"This is Heaven alright, but there's a man outside with a gun."
—Cardiacs, "What Paradise is Like"

TABLE OF CONTENTS

This book is dedicated to Alyssa Goncalves and Brian Warfield, who gave us the tools we needed.

Additional thanks to John Edward Lawson and Michael Allen Rose, for their amazing support from the beginning.

Special thanks to Amelia Gulbranson, for being our "bonus" five for this volume: don't worry, she'll be back.

And another eight million thanks to Matthew Revert, for this really fucking awesome book cover.

DLV
An Introduction by the Series Editor

The history of my involvement with the 55-word story is (mostly) brief and (very) boring, so I'll not waste the effort here. In summary, for the last four years, which I will humbly refer to as my "actually maybe giving a fuck about writing" years, one project idea has survived the endless cycle of not-enough-talent, not-enough-time, and not-enough-commitment: my desire to put out a collection of fifty-five stories, each exactly fifty-five words long.

Fast-forward to the autumn of 2014. Josh Myers, an amazing writer (read: hack) in his own right, convinces me to bring the project out of hibernation. He tells me he'll write up his own series of 55-word stories, and shit, maybe we can convince some others to do so as well. The end goal? 555 stories. Five-hundred fifty-five. Each exactly fifty-five words long.

The number is meaningless, there's no significance in five, or fifty-five, or five-hundred fifty-five. But dammit, the project is still *significant*.

We convinced the best writers we personally know and respect to tell us their best short-short stories, and they fucking delivered. How could they not? There'd be no book in your hands if not for their commitment to bringing you as many electrifying story ideas in as few words as possible. Their work transformed this concept from "Well shit, maybe we can do this," to *"Well shit, maybe we can fucking do this.*" In addition to everyone else thanked elsewhere in this volume, the nine authors who joined Josh and me on this venture deserve our infinite gratitude. There truly are none so worthy.

As the title of my section shamelessly suggests, this series is goddamn invincible. It will not stop! Stay tuned for more 5/five/55/555 shenanigans in upcoming volumes. Until next time!

Joseph Bouthiette Jr.
Somewhere, Somewhen
Spring 2015

GODDAMN INVINCIBLE

Joseph Bouthiette Jr.

For Andersen Prunty and Michael Arnzen

DRAQFT

Automated Postal System:
INSERT ENVELOPE HERE.
Bits of plastic, chunks of skin with sugar skull tattoos, rubber shavings, white pepper flakes, a board game meeple. DO NOT LICK ADHESIVE.

"Welcome to DRAQFT, home of the National Automated Postal System Bureau. All standard envelopes are frozen in methane ice before being set ablaze..."

PLEASE COME AGAIN.

THE MAN WHO STARES AT ANTS

The man who stares at ants crumbles cheddar cheese between his burnt fingertips and allows it to fall to the ground.

The ants do not mind.

The man who stares at ants removes his prosthetic legs and falls to the ground himself, shovelling dirt and crumbled cheese into his mouth.

The ants do not mind.

PIANO GIRL

Going to the dentist must be a whole new experience for you, Piano Girl, keys and teeth astray. Good maintenance goes hand in hand with good health, and as such, a good general well-being.

Anyways, you mentioned something about a dull ache? Open up. Aha! And there's your problem: your pain is under a fermata.

EVOLUTION OF THE CHASTITY BELT

He lifts up her skirt, and a solar flare discharges at near nova velocities, narrowly missing him. With the foresight of a scavenger, he leaves for a target with less combustive qualities. But the singes still remain at the edge of her evening wear. When she gets home, Father will be so proud of her.

CELEBRATE THE DEATH

Six pallbearers carry a coffin. One made of cardboard that reveals an empty interior. The contents fall into a shallow grave next to the fence. Six children celebrate the death of an imaginary friend. They laugh and kick dirt into the hole. They high-five and spit on each other and piss themselves. Their mothers weep.

VIOLA GIRL

Viola Girl, you're all the hype down at Natalie's Beauty Salon. The hairdressers there can't get enough of your tin string hair, the music it produces melodious and soothing. And let's not forget about fellow customers, who arrive at your appointments as if it were concert night.

You've gone with pigtails today: an excellent choice.

HARSH EVERYTHING

Silencing the clarion claxons by closing the hatch, I step from the submarine. I'm greeted by the smell of cat piss and cattle skulls bleached white by the sun and worn smooth by the sands. A robed figure stoops over a pile of rotting shark corpses. It raises its head.

I am not welcome here.

ICE FISHING

Barbed words of attraction fall from her mouth, and I fall for the bait. She pulls the line, fire in her eyes as I crash through the ice.

She stares. She laughs. She shrieks, "You're a fucking parasite!"

Naked in the bitter biting wind under an endless icy sky, I curl around my frozen heart.

NO REST FOR THE WICKED

She paints in the blood dripping from the two corpses hanging above her, greasy nooses cutting deep. One was her father, but her face bears no recognition of the fact. She playfully murmurs the last words she heard.

"There's no rest for the wicked, Jezebel."

But the syllables still form useless sounds in her ears.

RIDE-ON LAWNMOWER

He idles on hands and knees, and she straddles him bareback. He is entirely nude; she wears skin-tight, flesh-toned clothing.

He chomps and chews and crawls on the grass, occasionally pausing to lick his palms. She steers the awkward herbivore under a sun that never seems to set.

And the lawn has never looked better.

DANCING SHOES

With a white face and a scream, she pushes the stillborn clowns out. The doctor holds their umbilical cords like puppet strings and marches them in their amniotic polka dot sheen across her deflated abdomen, and I, the father, dance along with shoes far too small for my feet.

Now she screams with a smile.

PATCHES

The wall starts steaming. The white paint bubbles and sloughs off in patches, melting in the frigid hospital air. The whole wall trembles with restrained exertion, released as only a soft sigh. It stiffens once more.

Caroline stares. The IV feels tight in her arm.

"Dr. Callahan, please call 413. Dr. Callahan, please call 413."

HOW I LEARNED TO FLY

Maybe I'm losing weight, or maybe I'm losing my sense of the ground.

I'm stretching with the corn pounded into the wheat, a crop circle I'm levitating a leviathan over. I'm a steady diet of atmosphere, blue sky bones to lift.

I'm a sheep to my gravity's shepherd.

I pray.

And the continents follow suit.

KILL TONIGHT

We shoot down the freeway, blocked on three sides by fellow interstate commuters with no idea what sort of night they are in for.

On our left, the separating guardrail.

She turns and chuckles, "Let's kill tonight, baby."

I smile.

A sharp left. A screeching inferno.

And a bloody gash tears across the twilit sky.

THERE BE (CLOCKWORK) DRAGONS
(With respect to Dani Filth)

*"Write a story, any story,
but let there be dragons."*

I brought the golden staff to the village.

The firing of pistons, the shriek of crude bronze wing joints, the overwhelming scent of basalt and sulfur. Empty carcasses of apothecaries, haberdasheries, slaughterhouses. The beast lurks in ambush.

The staff vibrates in my gauntlet. It's ready.

MISERY MISHEARD

*"The Great and Secret Show
Glitters like the stars upon the festive snow"*

She brought The Great and Secret Show to my dimension, freak show antics and muted lights crossing the cosmic rift. The masks are awful and the screams tinged with hate, but it warms the limbs, even as they consume the naïve heart.

ICE FISHING II

I've been calling her Julia.

She's frightening; I want her. But she's beautiful, and I fear her. Something about her eyes, her smile...

Even encased in ice, she still smiles.

She's dangerous. Radioactive. Apocalyptic. As long as the ice holds, this aquatic terror, this antarctic nightmare, will be harmless. As long as the ice holds...

HALIBUT
(With respect to Josh Myers)

Josh paused at the halibut tank.

"We all have our problems, buddy."

After feeding the fish, he then returned to staring out the window. Few people passed, and none entered the aquatic pet store. Josh focused on his reflection in the glass instead, eyeballs aligned vertically down his right cheek.

"We all have our problems..."

MANSCAPING

With wide eyes, he presses his face into the pubic hair ceiling. Wiry bits and ends enter his pupils, which bite down and trim the garden around the daisies. He grows these trimmings into a beard, imposing masculinity even while tending to his flowers. The ceiling sweats a sweet musk, and his chomping pupils glow.

COMPARATIVE ANATOMY

He takes a large bite of his soft-shell crab sandwich, jaw clicking and forming irregular angles as he chews the crustaceous cud. His throat, his entire neck, expands to accommodate the swallow.

He reaches for a nearby napkin, and I nail his hand to the table with my fork. His blood looks nothing like mine.

THE AUDITION

She takes the stage, graceful with lithe limbs that seem to shift from this world to the next. She dips deeper and lower than her earthly body would have allowed. And when she jumps, she floats as if the gentlest of dandelion seeds.

She'll never be the lead.

But she won't stop until she is.

MISS DEMEANOR

"What does this do?" she asks. "What does the sun do? *What does the fucking sun do?* You're addicted to breathing. In cold blood. We stare at slaughtered women. Cock-breathed motherfuckers drinking drama and reading into the tragedy of gravity, stuck to the ground because the sky doesn't fucking want you and neither do we."

ODOROUS MARCH

Stilettos bore holes in the soft earth between patches of brittle moss clumps, and strands of her hair grow from the inlets, attracted to the conformity of her feet formed against red-clad heels, soles soft with sweat. Yet they remain held to the dirt by the root, tangled and swaying to her odorous march galore.

CONCEIT

"I love when your eyes are all over me. Makes me feel beautiful." She breathes a soft sigh as a tear rolls down my face. "Mmm, yes, I do love it."

She rolls off the bed and dons a robe. I return my withered eyes to their sockets and continue to cry. She walks away.

UDDER DELIGHT

Loaded shotgun in hand, Mary stomped towards the barn.

"Jack, you better hide your whore, or I'll blow a hole through her!"

Mary slammed the barn door open and discovered her husband naked under the cow, ravenously pulling at her teats and his pecker.

Mary blew a hole through the face on the milk carton.

THOSE WHO ABANDON

Black walls and purple stairs (climb/stretch) infinitely upward but never down(ward). Crow feathers litter the stairwell: those who abandoned them (now form the walls/now watch from above, ebony angels in an ebony heaven).

They wait.

I trip.

(A green face in the void/They tear each other apart).

And then it's all gone.

THE MOST BORING GLASS OF ORANGE JUICE

John went downstairs and grabbed a glass from his cabinet. He went to the fridge and poured himself some orange juice. He took a sip. Then another. And another. Soon, the glass was empty, and he placed it in the sink. From there, he grabbed a steak knife and plunged it into his eye socket.

STRIGIFORMES

Fingers pry through the concrete to reveal the small, winged locket. The case is scratched, revealing silver, or at least a silver metal, beneath the gold. The chain is broken, your blood flecked and dry.

I don't know when I lost it all if I lost control. But for you, an owl of any kind.

REGRET

The walls continue leaking, and Brittany continues sobbing.

"Please, mommy..."

The semen pools on the floor, enveloping her toes, ankles.

"I'm so sorry..."

A slight shiver when it touches her lady bits, infiltrates her, overwhelms her.

"Please," she gasps in orgiastic pleasure.

The room's blue haze shimmers as the baby broth surpasses her baby bump.

SPONTANEOUS GENERATION

My mouth is maggots. They bore through my collapsed face; they multiply and push through my soft, rotten skull.

Even sealed in glass, I'm a failure. Science frowns down on me through the lid.

But my maggot eyes look upon my maggot hands clenched to my maggot heart and smile a maggot smile for me.

MADE BY HUMANS

Fingers flit across piano keys that produce no sound: each white key a digit, each black key an operation, a function. Mathematics as high art.

Fingers fumble with the transparent plastic: a small calculator designed to look like a piano, each white key a digit, each black key an operation, a device made by humans.

THE SERRATED SISTERS

The ex-conjoined twins take their time cutting the child in half, absorbing every detail, every touch of tension. They go to work with razor-blades and electric saws and meat cleavers.

Abandoned by their whore mother at birth, charitable locals funded their separation.

The sisters had no say in being torn apart.

Neither do their victims.

LOVE STORY

Smiling, you drown me in love letters, each a razor edge. A paper cut for every paper heart, and I kiss each with a drop of red.

You drown me in your drinking. Alcohol cleans wounds, but the sting is always worse.

So I'll cry.

And you'll leave me a paper heart, a razor edge...

FLATTER THAN GRAVITY

She smothers me under pounds and pounds and absolute pounds of her heaving flesh. Waves of woman compress me like a fundamental elemental force, an event horizon bound by bed sheets, thrashing and humping and pulling and pushing. The steel bedposts audibly creak under the strain and somewhere down there is penetration and I'm choking.

THE PRIZE

"Remember, whoever finds the prize is up for dinner tomorrow night!"

And with that, everyone started feasting on the tasteless grey matter that lay oozing on their plates in front of them.

Suddenly, Andy exclaimed, "I found it!" as he raised a deformed bullet into the air.

The next shot went clean through his skull.

STAINED SHOES

Choking on her skin through the gasps.

Bits of cloth tossed in myriad direction, striking the desk, the mantle, missing the laundry hamper. Stained shirts, stained shorts, stained socks, a clean bill of health.

She writhes and deflates, dust bunny contraceptive.

And all the semen that should be on my sleek black shoes, but isn't.

OLD BONES

There's something in the water here, or maybe the air.

Smoke stacks sputter and spit in the distance while Basil desecrates the backyard. Holes follow her to Misty's unmarked grave, where she digs up root and rot. She chews on her old bones, dog eat dog, and they bite back.

Maybe it's in the soil.

THE UNDERLYING CODE OF ALL

Adam's legs stretched and deformed the higher he climbed the ladder. Step by step, the great ladder propelled towards an obscene moon. Space warped to reveal the infrared numbers beneath, incalculable derivatives manifesting in tangential streams of tetrahedral code, a physical oppression on Adam's breathing. The air got thinner, time got thinner, the moon exhaled.

THE WALTZ OF WIDOWS AND WIDOWERS

And they take synchronized steps to the tragic chords, each embracing none and dancing as if alone in the dusky ballroom. Their arms never grow tired as they waltz with ghosts long fled but never forgotten. Contact is never made; haunted edge always misses haunted edge, tuxes and dresses like lithe cobwebs gently floating about...

AND PUT DOWN YOUR VICIOUS SWORDS
(Again, for Filth)

Geometric illusions carved in pink chalk on concrete. She sprinkles essential salts and motor oil. She cuts her hand on precious swords and sprinkles what comes out.

She is naked, she is beauty, she takes steps under yellowing streetlights. She takes my hand and opens my meat face.

Befuddled by a new brand of witchcraft.

THE BURNING OF RAYCE

Flames reflect off the polished willow wood as they leap from column to marble column. Rayce sets the sandpaper aside and blows the dust from the face carved into the cello. It reflects his own face, tight-lipped and hollow-eyed. Embers rain upon him from the theater's rafters as he takes up his bow and plays.

MEDUSA PHOTO SHOOT

A row of portraits hangs upon the gallery wall, photographs enlarged and enhanced to perfect clarity. Each depicts a figure shrouded in a black cloak. Each is from a different angle, but never the front—the subject's face is never seen.

At the end of the set stands a statue, immaculate. It holds a camera.

AMPUTEE LOVE STAINS

I wake in a haze beside a lovely lady who's half the woman she ought to be. Red stains everything: the sheets.

Her gown.

My hands.

In her sleep, she runs from nightmares on ragged stumps. She hides her face with phantom hands.

I taste her missing limbs on my lips, my teeth, and smile.

WHITE FLESH

A single pillar of marble (white flesh and blue veins worn smooth by uninhabited waves, unmapped, unseen by temperate shore or towering fjord, uncarved by human hands or otherwise, unknown to its own titanic solitude, eternal, its prehistoric existence lost in the dawn of forbidden cosmic alchemy) pierces the tempest's throes.

Let there be light.

ICE FISHING III

A tear freezes on my face as the ice I'm carving takes shape.

A flounder. Just like she ordered those many years ago. But I never caught her name, and she's never returned.

So now I spend every freezing moment carving new flounders. And just maybe, she'll come back to me to pick it up.

SOMEDAY YOU'LL WISH THAT YOU COULD FLY

Young men in black t-shirts and beards push you around, screaming, "Tearing myself apart!" and "Poison in my *brain* driving me in*sane*!" You slip in the nectar leaking from their ears, from the milky welts in their skin. Sweet nostril caresses and brash tussling as you break free from the swarm.

The bees follow you.

CAPTAIN MANIAC SAVES THE DAY!

"Oh dear!" Jason says. "Dad's locked his keys in the car!"

"Maybe Captain Maniac will help!" Jennifer suggests.

Singing together, "Oh, Captain Maniac!"

Captain Maniac appears in the front seat, on fire, screaming. He pulls at his burning hair and kicks the door, unlocking it. He sobs once, nods solemnly, and disappears.

"Thanks, Captain Maniac!"

CAPTAIN MANIAC MAKES A FRIEND!

Spot the Dog runs a lap around the yard. He sniffs at Captain Maniac's pants. He pees on Captain Maniac's pants and runs back to Jason, calling him from inside.

"Hello, pee stain," Captain Maniac says to the pee stain. "Maybe we can be friends."

A hole opens beneath Captain Maniac and he falls forever.

CAPTAIN MANIAC
GOES TO THE PARK!

An updraft carries the kite into the closest elm tree.

"Oh no!" says Jason

"Golly!" Jennifer replies.

"NOW YOU FUCKED UP," cries Captain Maniac. "NOW YOU FUCKED UP. NOW YOU FUCKED UP."

A ballistic missile embeds him in the ground, the sonic boom dislodging the kite.

"Thanks, Captain Maniac!" They run off to play.

"Ohhhhh."

CAPTAIN MANIAC
COMES TO DINNER!

"Let us say grace, and be thankful for this meal," father says.

Jason and Jennifer fidget in their seat. Captain Maniac says, "Fuck you," and tosses the turkey at the wall. It bounces off the wall, leg bones piercing his eyes, then falls back onto its platter for carving.

"Amen," the family says in unison.

CAPTAIN MANIAC
DOES LAWN WORK!

Jennifer sits back on her heels and wipes the sweat from her brow. "Tending the garden is hard work!" she says.

A series of thumps is heard from the shed, and Captain Maniac tosses out his severed leg. Spot the Dog takes it and buries it in a corner of the garden bursting with blueberries.

CAPTAIN MANIAC
GETS A PEN PAL!

Jason lies on the floor reading a comic book. Jennifer brushes her doll's hair.

Captain Maniac drives a screwdriver through his palm and uses the bloody tip to carve *YOU DIRTY MOTHERFUCKER* into a clay tablet. He continues much the same way until he passes out from blood loss.

Jennifer giggles. "You're funny, Captain Maniac."

CAPTAIN MANIAC
GOES TO THE CHURCH PICNIC!

"You're a fucking disgrace!" Captain Maniac yells at church members from atop the cathedral. He waves his arms excitedly, trips.

Jennifer realizes she's forgotten her potato salad for the church picnic. She bites her lip, tugs at her mom's skirt, quietly asking to return home for it.

Captain Maniac hits the ground and stays there.

TO WATER

A dromedary camel trots along the dunes of a jovian desert. Red hurricanes blister the horizon. Moons expel crystalline gases and collide.

A single probe, once polished to a mirror sheen, now pitted with meteorite strikes and worn dull from sandstorms, gently floats behind the camel's sways, transmitting video to a population no longer watching.

SKULL SLUMBER SUSPENSION

My bedroom is a gallows. A bent wire dangles from the ceiling, mocking slumber and sanity.

My eyelids are heavy but will not close, not until I have the wire...

So I climb my stool and feed the wire through my skull, my jaw hinge. With clenched teeth, I kick the stool away.

Sleep tight.

BLACK FIRE UPON US

Jess Gulbranson

For my family.

A special thanks to Dr. Susan Gritzner, for "The Pumpkin". Based on a true story.

THE VEXILLOLOGY DEPARTMENT: INTRO

"I'm not sure you are even aware of the Scunthorpe Problem," intoned the vexillologist. "It does not matter how we justify the text, or what typeface we use. The word 'cunt' becomes too prominent. It ruins the design." Hard lines were cut into his gray face. Faded flags lined the walls of his dingy office.

DEMON CLEANER

Flight... the dream of men since before dreams. Leaping, soaring, gliding on the breeze... and not just in a dream.

I've assembled these potions for you, as I know you to be a discerning consumer. There are no miscibility worries, I assure you.

These are your standard quaffs... except for the flying potion, of course.

TIGER DETENTION CENTRE

Henk Trejver was not the sort of man to take defeat lightly, and when he discovered that an old tattoo of his had slipped a bit and gotten away from the calf it lived on, he knew he would never rest until he had caught that wayward ink and returned it.

"Is it behind me?"

UNION SCALE

At the craft table he was almost afraid to talk to her, and he ended up not saying much.

"You've got a great voice."

She was unimpressed with him: just out of a relationship, puffy, not much sleep. Unclear motivations. But the inverse was definitely true. She was the pale redhead, striking features. Background unclear.

THE QUEEFING MANIAC

Look, I don't mean any disrespect. I understand that you are just doing your job. I get that. I'm not one of those mouthy customers that's looking for something to complain about. But I have my dignity, and I will not give my lunch order to someone whose nametag says *THE QUEEFING MANIAC*. Final word.

THROMBOR THE BARBARIAN FACES HIS ARCHFRENEMY

Thrombor faced the arrayed armies. Soldiers occupied the pass before him in gleamingly armored rows as far as the eye could see. At the head of the horde was General Limaxicus, face red with rage. His gold-braided uniform sparkled as he screamed.

"I WILL DESTROY YOU, THROMBOR!"

"Not in that atrocious outfit you won't, whispertits."

THROUGH THE EYE OF TERROR

The following commercial is brought to you by Amalgamated Goat Corporation, maker of fine goats and goat-related entities. Ask for AGC everywhere goats are sold.

Closed-captioning provided by Fantod Limited. This holiday, what will you have under glass?

A consideration has been made by the Veteran Beggar's Guild, in honor of St. Swithin's Feast Day.

CHLORINE TRIFLOURIDE

The letter was surprising, both for its content and its appearance. The address was unfamiliar, city and street in a configuration obviously foreign. The postmark indicated origin, or at least processing in "Republic of Taured". None of it was remotely familiar. Of course, the threatening nature of the letter itself was taken into serious consideration.

SWEET REFUGE

Ahh, the Gunners' Rose. Not an emblem I've seen in a long time. Could find a buyer for it, of course, if we had time, which we don't. So what will you take in trade? I've plenty of the standard stuff, but if you're looking to dump the Gunners' Rose? Trade for a 55th Kettleblack?

XI BALBA

This is where you are, the table, the table-cloth, the missingno, the Ben Drowned, the flat beer and glasses of bitter rose-colored water, the flapping robes of a fleeing priest, the lute, the lute-based seduction, the lube, the morning after, the omelette, the slammed door, the motherfucking lute music.

This is where you are, man.

A MIND FOR TRAPS

Racheheit was surprised at the sheer quantity of donuts, but disappointed in the lack of variety. He'd killed so many to get here, would it have killed them to include some custard-filled, or one of those crumbly old-fashioned kind? He'd be damned before he'd eat a maple bar. Thrice damned. He would. He so would.

GUNS OF THE LOBSTER NEBULA

Esquire hadn't had any problems in the Blazing Quadrant since she destroyed the Palatine Navy's space fleet—with them still in the docks. And she had her pick of the wenches at Elohim Station. But there was something missing, and it didn't take mutant telepathy to guess—some other space pirate was gunning for her.

SATAN'S VERY OWN
HOT PUBLIC TESTICLE

Where to then the steersman, enjoining thrustwise such signs
Done and donated in those open spaces west and further west
Crammed of steel caverns mood thing bedecked
Devil you know not know how the swarm accumulated members in twain
Haddock shouters tell no dead names of heaven's tail
Dwerrow armaments supplied north
A reasonable suggestion

INVENTORY

Dead medicine and spiked coffee, a hitlist of perverts thrown into the street. Pegged pants and vintage kukris. Empty pomade cans reused as containers for knocked out teeth. A burlap sack for throwing over a pervert's head, and one of those dense rubber fish-killing clubs for beating their faces in. Cigars dipped in embalming fluid.

DEMURRAGE

The crate was full of chicken oysters. This was understandably confusing to the staff at the loading dock, considering they shipped industrial machines and missile guidance system gimbals. It took a full day to even determine the provenance of the crate, and by 9:00 there was already a union grievance over the amount of demurrage.

SECRET OF DEVIL CAVE

"Dance with me." Little black dress. Husband watching. Nice guy. Lucky man.

"Nope." He looks at hubby. They share a weird wordless masculine smile. Back at her, pale skin set against the dress, her slim body. He imagines her heels digging into the back of his thighs, her fingernails at his back. "I don't dance."

IF YOU'RE NASTY

Open eyes, dim light coming through the window, night cloud-smudge focused through the gap between air conditioner and pane. The air is thick, still as he attempts to lift his head, greasy pain shoots from his shoulder, through his temple, and out his eye socket. He half expects lightning past his tear-stained vision. It ain't.

THE LEAST OF ALL MY DISCIPLES

He felt like that. Boxed in by tolex, breathing heavily through a cat-clawed tweed barrier. Suffocating. Hot ozone at his head. Finger oils warmed by friction, roundwounds grinding on ebony fingerboard, black dust on harness boots that had been replaced by the sooty remnant of solid forklift tires, on more sensible off-brand sneakers. Fucking foundering.

WALL MEAT

I find it hard to understand why she rejects these overtures: what choice does she think she has? The cleats in the brick wall are strong, and the chains so attached are thick and unbreakable. I littered the stairs out of the basement with broken glass. It doesn't trouble my boots any. Bare feet, though...

WHENCE CAME

One day, taking their leave, he led his girlfriend out of Troy's house, onto the street. He loved to hold her hand, loved to take spontaneous walks, lean in close, stroke her stomach, take in her smell. The leather of her jacket. Tobacco and gum from her purse. A dab of patchouli. And... somehow, gunpowder.

THE PUMPKIN

"It's my very own design."

She pointed to the whiteboard, on which a terrifying runic mess had been described. Each curving line, each criss-cross was heavily scrawled, as if in haste. And all those lines terminated in glyphs that represented every aspect of human suffering. It hurt to look at.

"I call it... *The Pumpkin.*"

BENTHIC REGION

The extent of the corruption at this institution is amazing. I asked to meet here in the library because it is quiet and discreet, but as you can hear two rows over, they are filming a reverse bukkake scene. I can barely hear myself think. Imagine how bad it is on the weekends. I'm through.

DECRET

Sleep. When he wakes up, she is breathing steady and slow. His vision swims and her tattoos crawl with the shadows, along her arm, up her spine, past the curve of her ass, and onto the bed. The tattoos climb the wall, slip under the door. The neighbors' music fades in and out, conjunto.
Sleep.

MOIDAH

"How is the writing?"
"Fine," she said. "Just got some poetry in a couple journals." She leaned her head against his chest. He let his clasped hands slip down the small of her back, past the end of her shirt, resting finally against the swell of her ass. And...
"Are you seeing anyone?" She nodded.

AKSHOBYA

They named her Akshobya, and what a name that was. Her primary purpose as a neighborhood infiltrator was obscured by the sock hop outfit they'd attired her in, at least until Halloween, where candy was free and memories short. Then the body count started to rise, and people started to pay attention.

She was unstoppable.

MEMORY

She was the dictator, the lover, the pilot. That's always how it's been. Things remained simple. He remained simple. Get from the threshold to bed in as few steps as possible.

How else to honor her?

But how can you be free if you are so many people? What would you do with that freedom?

THE VEXILLOLOGY DEPARTMENT: INTERMISSION

The vexillologist makes a sweeping gesture across the factory floor, and with his free hand wiped away a pretend tear.

"Look at them. So beautiful." He notices my gaze. The gleaming chests of the newly-minted robots are emblazoned with a curious set of symbols.

"So..."

He rubs his hands together vigorously. "Significant, my boy. Significant."

THE KING'S EVIL

Welcome, imps. This may not be your chosen haunt, but I hope the accommodations will be to your liking. The pickings are, as they say, plentiful. Just don't open the red door. You'll be sorely surprised if you do. What happened to the last set of imps? Well, find out. I'll just be waiting here.

APPROACH THE THRONE

In the sandwich of death it was stone-ground mustard. On the vehicle of conflict it was the mustard-flavored axle. In the band of trauma it played a five-string mustard-colored bass. In the sandwich of life it was motor oil. On the vehicle of peace it was artisan bread. In the band of solace, upright ham.

THE SUIT

Cedric flailed in his high-temperature lava suit. It was exquisitely uncomfortable, and quite hot. He fumbled at the latch of the helmet, hoping to let some fresh air in, but the suit's mittens were too clumsy.

He heard Sue's muffled shouting.

"Cedric! You put it on wrong! Lava goes on the outside of the suit!"

CLOTHO NO LACHESIS

There were ten footholds up the cliff and Racheheit missed just one. As he tumbled down the abyss, brisk air rushing through his clothes and an unseen ground approaching, there was just one thought in his mind: had the donuts at the top of the cliff been a lie? Were there donuts at the bottom?

WISE WORDS, MY FRIEND

If you want a Clovis point in the balls, then take one step closer. I double dog fucking dare you.

You want to talk? Good. Fine. But you don't talk with your feet, do you? Then stand the fuck still.

What? No. Anything you can say to me, you can say to her.

Be careful.

LITTLE JIMMY OSTERBERG REVEALS
THE INVADERS' FIVE YEAR PLAN

Months among the dirty Crenshaws had honed his senses. All but smell, of course. The dirty Crenshaws lived up to their name by reeking of burnt deep fry oil, asscrack vinegar, and strangely, fenugreek. This last odor, a sickly sweet essence of syrupy waffles, was enough to make a hard man cry. And cry he did.

THE NORWEGIAN IS A
SHREWD ENTREPRENEUR

There were a lot of knockoff Idiots, mostly either considerably cheaper than the original or claiming a larger suite of features, but were always of inferior quality. The Norwegian rarely enforced his rights, unless one of the fugazi Idiots had a good idea or decent innovation. Then he'd steal it with no hesitation at all.

VAUXHALL

Run run run. You sneaking crow. You thieving crow. You fucking magpie. Go shit in your boot and eat it. You fuck. You dirty motherfucker. There isn't enough piss in the world to drown your big mouth. I hope you trip and fall through your own asshole and break your motherfucking neck. Eat my balls.

SPRING-HEELED JERSZY

I've always wondered why it was so hard to walk down the street. Don't get me wrong, I have nothing against the street, or the people on it. I don't.

Forgive me. These last years have been hard on me as a travelling preacher. Jumping from rooftop to rooftop is no way to gain a congregation.

EXTEMPORANEA

We were entranced, like two potatoes in love: all eyes and tendrils. The dome of smog rose luridly that day and portended strained conversations in Pan-Asian supermarkets. Death before dishonor, not just a suggestion, but the law. Deadly turtles, snapping beaks dipped in poisonous resin. We were followers of a narrow way, a shining path.

ROPE ROPE ROPE

Rope rope motherfucking rope. Rope rope not enough rope. Rope rope give them enough rope. Rope rope coils of rope. Rope rope coils of rope. Rope rope hoist up that rope. Rope rope rope a dope. Rope rope a necktie made of rope. Rope rope funny old rope. Rope rope the king's finest rope. Rope.

BUMP CITY

This right here is how you make a great Coney Island. First, you need meat for the sauce. This is the most important part. And it has to simmer for too long in a red sauce with no reasonable provenance. Next, chopped onions. Especially if the customer asked for no onions. Then serve that shit.

THE FORGOTTEN FOLIO

Racheheit could not believe that his rival, Herr Rucksack, had preceded him in this competition. A head start was an enormous tactical advantage, not even counting the psychological advantage it gave. This inequity was not insurmountable, of course, and Racheheit would fuck blazes through this town's whorehouses like his life depended on it. It did.

THE GRIP OF A TYREFITTER'S HAND

The first person I talked to was a stand-up comedienne carrying a cardboard box full of Pink Floyd t-shirts. After the shoot, I managed to end up with the redhead on my lamp, her huge, soft ass smothering my balls and her patchouli giving me a headache. That was the first time. Not the last.

NONE SO BRAVE

hellion then when the metal skin flexes for the whelping
then
when the skin redoubles and loses flex
the sin is real
korinski agrees with everything that has been said so far
the lore is well-documented with significant corroboration
downtown
whores chase priests through light-bombed cloisters
boys chase girls
then tell me
who was it?

THE CITY RESTS UNEASY

The city turned over during its nap and spilled its bong on the floor. The city was unable to get the smell out of the cheap rug it bought at Ikea. The city squatted obscenely like leprous fungi after rain. The city told its girlfriend a white lie about where it went right after work.

THIS HOUSE

This house is homey and comfy. Everyone who comes over remarks how warm and inviting the kitchen is. There is always a pot of myrrh tea on. A kitschy welcome mat has already greeted the guests, who have wiped their feet. The walls are decorated in a tasteful pattern of dead ghost hunters. Our house.

DRY BONES

The heat has gone out of this land, and its citizens drop like flies. I have my duties, and I must trudge up and down the ruined stairs and ramps. My cold flesh has done me no favors, and my feet have worn down to dry stubs.

Send me a sign. That's all I'm asking.

THROMBOR'S VICTORY

Thrombor threw a haymaker with his scarred right fist, downing one of the tavern's bravos. With his other, he swung his dreaded vibrating mace, which smashed the nearest table to flinders and scattered the last standing fighters. With nobody left to challenge him, he called towards the bar.

"Barkeep, a Sea Breeze for victorious Thrombor!"

RIPARIAN

Bill blew a snort to the side and took a deep breath. These motherfuckers had raided his orchard for the last time.

Call it... certainty, or fatalism, but Bill knew it ended here. Filberts crunched as he rose from a crouch, firing his rifle as he revealed himself. They died, he fired. Again.

"Fucking gophers!"

GOLD AND GOLD

Well, this is it. Make your beds and your sandwiches. The punting blunt sends an appropriate signal. Woe to you, earth and sea. Here is the hearing. An oi band destroys a pub. A donkey rebuilds it. The phone rings, and a man answers. You are too sensitive to initial conditions. You catty fucking bitch.

PENCIL DICK

hey you pencil neck geek

hey

listen here it is the way things are going to be unless you fuck it up again like the time before i can't believe you fucked a jazz musician don't you remember mom warning us about that

god don't even pretend you don't know what i'm talking about

hey

ROTATOR COIFFE

The first flashpot exploded with only minor consequences, but it did serve to distract the lead singer, who stumbled, thankfully not on fire, into a nearby bank of pyros, which fell pointing towards the audience. He continued his unintentional pratfall, activating the spring-mounted spike canisters, which did release into the eager faces of the crowd.

SERIOUS BUSINESS

I squeezed the rubber bulb. The material depressed between my fingers, but when I released the pressure, the squashed bulb returned precisely to its original shape. I repeated the operation and was surprised to find the same results. While this occurred, I noticed an itching sensation appear on the skin of my unlotioned left leg.

OXIDE DOG POUND

"Ms. Taliaferro, I appreciate you giving me a chance to test these canine translation collars at your shelter. Shall we? You do the honors. That button there."
"LET ME TELL YOU ABOUT YOUR M—"
"EAT TEN DICKS!"
"EAT TEN BAGS OF DI—"
"NO, YOU."
"YOU DONE FUCKED UP N—"
"GUEST OR HOST?"
"YOU DIRTY MOTHERFUCKER."

SELTZER WATER FACE CLOWN

Whelped at the fountain of death, the fountain of lemonade. The curses. Excellent timing, yes? There is only one thing to know. One thing you must know. This you must remember. Bells pealing. And then we continue. The legacy. As it should be. All the way down. I tell you again.

I am the devil.

DEATH TO ALL FANATICS

In the role of wacky neighbor, Grimsley Quade. In the role of angry female boss, Calpurnia Russelo. In the role of good-natured satanist, Donovon Morrivunt. In the role of annoying second cousin, Leslie Taupe. In the role of gold-digging exercise partner, Crash O'Dougal. In the role of lesbians, Bethany and Sue Ormion. And starring:

YOU.

THE VEXILLOLOGY DEPARTMENT: OUTRO

A robust smell of burning meat flooded the room, its contents barely distinguishable. Through tear-stung eyes, a few things were visible: slabs of carcass on hooks, metal grills over trays of burning coals, and at the back, a surprising figure... the vexillologist.

"You see," he said, holding a woman's arm. "All's well that ends well."

PURPLE VENGEANCE

William Pauley III

BECOMING A MOON

You see her there, say nothing, be nothing. She stands and the air around you disappears, you're choking, gasping. She walks, you spin, gasping, gasping. Seeing nothing but light, she wanders, bathing inside it, you slide forever into her shadow. You're comfortable. You've accepted. She walks, you spin, gasping, gasping. She walks, you spin, gasping.

SCREAMING AT THE EDGE
OF A BROKEN SEA

I never dream, but if I did, I'd imagine it'd be a lot like screaming, vomit and ash flying out from my mouth and nostrils in waves, in waves, in oceans moving fast, stretching over the sands, into the streets, flooding the earth and everything outside it. There is no room for space in dreaming.

NEVER BE TOO HARD TO KILL

Don't protect yourself from outside forces. Let it happen. Let something happen to you. Don't be afraid of anything. Let it come at you and kill you. Let knives inside you, let bullets penetrate your skull. Never stand there shielded. Never have control. Never fucking never. Goddamn it, for once in your life, be brave.

HUMAN NATURE IS NO LONGER HUMAN NOR NATURE

Progress is subjective. They define it differently, as a fact. They want to understand every part of everything. They want to know how it all works. They want to replicate and create and destroy, all at once and immediately. They wish to become god and to kill gods. We'll all be different soon.

Evolution, created.

DYING IN A SPRINT

I rarely stop to take a breath, and I know this will eventually kill me. The world is too exciting for rest. There are too many books, too many words, too many ideas, and faces and paintings and beaches and stars. The world is swarming and I don't want to stop breathing, but eventually will.

I LAUGH BECAUSE
WE ARE ALL NOTHING AND
YOU THINK YOU'RE SOMETHING

All of us are dust in a sneeze, and you're standing there, dying hair and singing in perfect pitch, eating the right foods and clipping toenails in a straight line, wearing jewelry, saving for cars, houses, vacations. Life is a series of distractions keeping us from remembering we are not important to anyone but ourselves.

SOME PEOPLE SAY I'M PARANOID, DON'T THEY?

There's a girl that lives down the road and she never says hello or smiles. Her eyes are the greyest green and her skin tastes metallic. When I touch her, she closes her eyes and thinks of someone else. She asks me to touch, taste and explore her body, but never says hello or smiles.

CLOTHING THE NAKED EYE

"The night tastes like electricity," she said and went inside to brush her teeth. He looked up at the moon, installed wires into it and flipped the switch. She said she loved a full moon, so he gave it to her. She didn't even bother looking when he told her. She'd be giving up soon.

SELF-PORTRAIT

Tried to paint a picture of you, but all I had was black and white. You're so colorful. I can't substitute emptiness for something so full of life. So I made a self-portrait instead, chest up to the head. Black eyes, busted tooth, black tongue sticking straight at you. You smile bright oceans of white.

LIFT

I can't get free from this parade. The sounds, the lights, have left me silent. It's getting to me. I need a barricade. The flames, the smoke, have left me burning. I can't be me. I need to behave. The shadows, the lights, have left me needing. If a hand were to reach, I'd break.

ANGELHORNS & DEVILTROMBONES

There is something very wrong here. Finger blades and a song of sorrow will bury us in our graves. Bullets will sound the sirens. Lightning will guide the way. Everyone who went without are now leaders in this war. Beggars be kings, down no more. Angelhorns and Deviltrombones will sound the end of an era.

A GLIMPSE

I sift through my pockets and unlock the car door. I push the key into the ignition, but wait to turn the engine. A memory finds me: her scent, her skin. I can almost feel her sitting next to me. I catch a glimpse, but she's already gone. I turn the key. Car barely starts.

DEVIL'S DAY

I'm not certain as to why the world is focusing so much on present matters. We should all be preparing for the not-too-distant future. Beasts, that as of now only exist in fairy tale, will be storming the land with a hunger for human flesh. The devil's out there waiting. Surely someone feels his presence.

SKIN

I'm not trying to forget, I'm trying to move on. My only light comes from the road, dear. Your skin keeps me here, keeps me feeling. My skin keeps you wanting, keeps you open, keeps you full. I'll stop looking back if you stop looking back. Our only light should come from the road, dear.

BREAK SAID SILENCE

I'm keeping record now. Where I've gone is so unclear, but where I am is so understood. You're gone. Of course you're gone. But you're always in my head, peeking through the blinds. I've always wanted to call you mine.

Your eyes are never honest, but still they're taking me, just like they always will.

ECHOES

Hands to wall. Slide your fingers down, love. Eventually you'll find your way out, but don't feel you have to leave so soon. You're swimming in me, just as I am swimming in you. Drowning even. And we love it. Lungs filling to the brim. When you're gone, we will continue drowning ourselves in others.

SLEEPTALKER

I almost always fall asleep before her, but nights when I'm awake long after, I listen. She talks to me in her sleep. She tells me things I could never see, could never dream. I run four long fingers through her dark hair, kiss her eyes and smile. Soon after, it's my turn to go.

COMFORTABLE

She and I, our minds are at work. Our hands are full of art. We know why we smile. Music fills our hearts. She knows my voice, and I know her skin like a doctor knows medicine. I take her in just as she takes me. We drink from our glasses until they are empty.

THE PIANO

The devil be hiding. His bones be the keys. The woman be playing black notes with weak knees. If angels be calling, then they be deaf to the ear, for the devil be shouting. These broken chords keep her near. The woman still singing, still swimming in fear. The devil still howling, still painfully clear.

THE RUINS

My cigar smoke breath whispers no more. Steadily I twist and bend, perfecting my bullshit design and yours, since you gave up long ago. We're just a blur, you and I, a flash of light fading before eyes of millions. Yet somehow we manage to have a good day now and then, but we're losing.

DEATH TO DEATH

Sights become ideas become words. Words to books to sight to ideas to words to words to words. Words to speech to ideas to words to books to sight to ideas to words to speech to ideas in both healthy and ill brains to words to speech to death to death to death to death.

SOMEONE IN AMERICA FIRED A GUN

To Americans, the gun is romantic. People come and go, but the gun is always near. A gun will never fail you, and to touch her skin is to feel power, instant power. She'll charge your veins with adrenaline long after you've become bored with your wives and husbands. And best of all, she's free.

DEATHDREAM

And in the night, the air hangs with a certain heaviness and a salty taste that could only ever be reproduced in the heart. The night air is biological, something that can be touched and taken in, though if you do you will surely dream of death and a deathdream is no way to live.

THIS SHIT IS THE FUTURE

We have the entire world at our fingertips. Our friends, our family, in our pockets. Films and music of every kind can be ours with a single click. We're getting nicotine fixes from electrical devices that run on batteries. The sunlight hurts our eyes the days we see it and that's exactly what they want.

MOON IS AUTOMATIC

She is lovely but sometimes we don't speak for days. There are moments I feel sick knowing she's out there and I'm in here, curled up, fingers bleeding, working for this. She breaks the silence every now and then, asking me to look at the moon. In different cities we still share the same sky.

DESERT FORGETS STRANGER

She tells me the desert is a mistake and it's too late to make it right, but I disagree. The savage sun wasn't meant for her fair skin and her long hair sticks to her face and friends are gone and she's alone. I ask her what she expects from the desert and she cries.

HUNG BY NIGHTMARE

Sometimes I wake in a paralyzed state. I see things around me that are both real and unreal, though it's hard to tell one from the other until I am completely awake and functional. Nightmares. It gets me wondering if I've ever been fully conscious at all. There are closed doors upstairs that need exploring.

LIFE IN A SMALL TOWN

Dee held her baby in her arms and told me her mother attempted suicide the week before. She almost smiled when she said it. Her mother was asleep in the chair beside us. Her own snoring often woke her. I stood to leave and kissed Dee goodbye. Our second kiss would be at the funeral.

A BIRD ON A STRING

A bird was hanging by a string in my front door this morning. It was still alive, but weak from struggle. It hung there, still, wings outstretched, as if already dead. I cut it loose and it flew. Hours earlier I was writing about Satan, and it got me wondering if the two were connected.

AN EVIL IN NASHVILLE

Last night we sped like a bullet shot from a cocaine straw straight into the hellish town of Nashville, Tennessee. We drank Mexican Coke at a place called Nervous Charlie's and spent the evening bathed in devil music. The lights of the city hung dangerously close. Nashville was on fire. Goddamn, the smoke was brutal.

A THOUSAND CREEPING FINGERS

I am distracted by light. I'm an insect, just as we all are insects. The more I realize and accept this, the faster I work, the faster my little insect digits type. I will continue to spit ink onto pages until all these goddamn creatures crawling around in my brain are gone. Words are parasites.

A LIGHT THAT NEVER GOES OUT

People never leave you, they become part of you, melt into you. Everyone you've ever loved is still lurking within you. No matter who you think you are, there's still part of your mind's canvas that is blank, untouched by others, 100% clean. Keep that part for yourself. Now get to work, and never stop.

TOTAL FUCKING SADNESS

I listened to the president's comments on Syria last night. We're killing to punish people that kill. Today is my four year old's first day at his new school. I woke him up playing The White Stripes' "We Are Going to Be Friends". My world and the world outside these walls couldn't be more different.

SWALLOWING MY GODDAMN TEETH

I've been crushed by a wall. Sometimes I feel the collaborative effort of others as they try rescuing me from tragedy [little hands reaching into the rubble and tossing whatever bricks they can to the side]. Sometimes I don't feel anything at all. I don't know which is worse, feeling the weight or the abyss.

MY SICKNESS

I stand under artificial light, absorbing energy, feeling more awake now. I spend nights alone, cramming information into my brain. When she comes downstairs in the morning, I spew information into her face and she bats it away, curls herself on the couch. I open the refrigerator and try my damnedest not to crawl inside.

MODERN GUILT

There are places that bleed, places where buildings breathe, and the surrounding air is being exhaled from their hot stinking mouths. Some places are dying. Other places are already dead. ___________________ chooses what places live and what places die. We can fill the blank, point fingers, but you know we only have ourselves to blame.

SOMETHING VACANT

A man with one cold blue eye stopped me walking down the street today.

He never looked at me in our strange moment together. His one blue eye wandered, connecting with the sky. He coughed and said, "Fuck you." He and I are made of the same electric human lunar shit. We are all one.

A PERFECT VISION WITH NO HOPE

As the airplane was spinning, speeding to the earth, I heard a sound. My son came to me and muttered something before disappearing completely: "How?"

I thought about the word, how powerful it was—enough to be a complete sentence. I started to answer, but he was safe in bed and dreaming all of this.

MY SUDDEN HAPPINESS

HA HA HA HA HA HA HA HA HA HA HA HA HA
HA HA HA HA HA HA HA HA HA HA HA HA HA
HA HA HA HA HA HA HA HA HA HA HA HA HA
HA HA HA HA HA HA HA HA HA HA HA HA HA
HA HA HA

GREAT FOG

Someone left the door open to this place and in the night came a bad fog. Been here since Friday or so. I manage okay. I've lived in fog before. However, now when I open the windows, more fog comes barreling in. Even on clear days, fog the instant the windows or doors open. Peculiar.

THE CRACKED NOBODY

He washes his hands before every meal and is thankful for all that is good. When the sun rises and warms his face, he opens his eyes and is grateful for another day. He never asks, and is always polite, and people smile when they hear his name, but not a single soul knows him.

COLD VISION

She couldn't see through doors or walls and never bothered wondering what worlds were on the outside. Others found her odd, but swore she was content. They walked their roads, and all winter brought was death. She never knew for sure, but outside she feared was heaven, and she was never good enough for that.

THE FLAMES OF HEALING

The glass was cold, and she held her face against it knowing it was sharp and dangerous. She dared it to move, to slide inside her. It seemed easier than doing it herself. It remained still, and her pain grew so she walked into the flames and only there was she able to find peace.

A MENTAL ABYSS

The human mind is a pit, empty at birth and filled with framed pictures of personal experience from top to the darkest realms of the bottom. Music echoes and statues often speak, reminding us of words spoken by others. All of this rearranged when dreaming. Some people are trapped inside it, others are ignorantly happy.

LEGEND OF EYE

There was a strange light coming through the leaves and when she saw it, she couldn't look away. He told her it was Eye, that it would sometimes manifest as bright rays of light, quick and sharp, and enter the psyche of onlookers through their pupil. She wouldn't have believed it had she been her.

SHARDS OF SPIRIT

He found a shard of spirit, and as he walked he found more. He gathered them up delicately and stacked them neatly, clutching them tight in his hand. He walked and gathered quickly and soon enough he found the woman they were breaking off from. He handed her the shards, but she refused to mend.

A WINDOW

It's been said that a man's house is a window to his mind. Mine is mostly warm, but certain rooms are drafty and cold. Things I love surround me, though I often get bored with it all. Some rooms are not finished, yet many of them have been ready for years. I hate it here.

WOMEN

He gave her a ring bought with his life savings and she took it knowing it was his heart and cried tears she felt were real and smiled in a way she never had before and when he drove her home they kissed deeply, but inside she hid it away, wearing only when he knocked.

LIGHTHOUSE MAN

"I see your problem right here," the doctor said, putting away his otoscope. "You've got a giant hole in your head."

"Oh yeah," the man said, not asking for an explanation or offering his own.

The man went home, lit a candle and slid it inside the hole. Next month's electric bill was dramatically lower.

AVOIDING THE RIVER

A swarm of bees carried me over the water and into a land with an abandoned landscape where empty skyscrapers lined along the horizon like soldiers in a halted march. Whispers hung in the air, though I couldn't decipher the words through all the buzzing. Never knowing haunted me for the rest of my days.

BOUND TO A STORM

Purple lightning strobed across the glittering night sky, connecting with the earth as close as twenty feet from me. Holding the wheel tight, I sped through the rain straight into the heart of the storm. There was a misunderstanding, a miscommunication that could only be rectified by skin, so straight into the heart I drove.

NEXT YEAR'S WOLF

"I've spent the last three years of my life being devoured," she said. "And a decade before that, but by other dogs."

He nodded, remaining silent.

"I've heard it all before, you see," she said. "Beasts, they know the same words as you, dear."

He spent the next three weeks sniffing before his next feast.

ROBOTS IN HEAVEN

He was late for the meeting, but he was the only one in attendance that could answer the question at hand: How can we make heaven more attractive to the living?

"We need to become more artificial," he said. "Humans are no longer impressed by natural wonders."

God nodded, giving creative control to the engineers.

THE BUTCHER OF DREAMS

Every morning I wake with blood smeared across the pillows, every orifice of my head bleeding. And every night I dream, but the trauma I suffer causes me to forget. There's a butcher of dreams that comes to those with guilt, and it comes for me though I try desperately to forgive and be forgiven.

BECOMING THE VULTURE

At the beach, I was a child then, I remember the sounds of waves crashing and a bird eating something dead on the sand. Growing older, the sounds of waves became the sounds of trains and everything in me felt dead in the sand. But now I'm even older, and looking back, I'm the vulture.

HIC SUNT BREVITAS ATROCITAS

Gabino Iglesias

SIDS

The baby won't stop crying. Greg sits in front of his computer and listens to the endless screams coming from the next room. He knows the only way to make it stop is to pick little Adam up and rock him for a bit. Unfortunately, he can't. Little Adam's been dead for a year now.

TRUCK

Sebastian picked up a colorful toy truck from a shelf and looked at the price. He frowned. The emptiness in his wallet was becoming a sucking void that threatened to swallow him. Then he understood that, more than not having for yourself, true pain comes from not being able to give to those you love.

THE LAW

He did what he wanted to do and felt no better. He stuck his dripping, sticky hand in his right front pocket and pulled out the crumpled piece of paper he'd been carrying around for six years. He read it for the zillionth time: "Do what thou wilt shall be the whole of the Law."

BUTTERFLIES

Maria never believed in magic until she met an old woman at the park who blew on her dress and made the butterflies on it come to life and fly away. Sadly, the butterflies came back that night, escaping the cold, and tried getting back into their home when Maria was not wearing the dress.

VERY WET DREAMS

"Yeah, and she had huge tits!"

Sammy's enthusiasm felt like a tumor inside Rick's chest.

The boys blabbered on about pussies and tits, which they'd never seen except on a screen.

Then the dreaded question came: "You have any dreams lately, Rick?"

Yeah, he had. Wet dreams, too. All of them about a giant octopus.

OLD MAN

The old man likes to go down to the park. He sits on a green bench and throws crumbs of stale bread on the ground. People walk by and smile at him. Parents tell their toddlers to say *hi* to the grandfatherly figure. The old man smiles, waves back, and dreams of devouring their flesh.

THE CURE

"I don't think this is a good idea," she says.

"Don't worry, baby," he replies, a warm smile plastered on his face.

"Is it dangerous?"

Her question makes him chuckle.

"The only dangerous thing in this world is ignorance. This cures you of that."

She trembles.

He smiles and pushes the needle into her arm.

YEAH, LIFE'S LIKE THAT, JACK

There once was a man who did his homework and paid attention and took notes in college and demonstrated all the right skills at his internship and landed a great job. He paid his bills on time and provided for his family. Then he got cancer and died because life is unfair. Go have fun.

YOU

Listen to me, you stupid asshole, I have something to tell you. Better listen up, you mammering fat-faced maggot. You yeasty foul-smelling flap-mouthed foot-licker. You failed superb opportunity to demonstrate the benefits of abortion. You lumpish idle-headed brute. You impertinent swag-bellied piece of garbage. You warthog faced buffoon. You snot-nosed under-developed monkey. I love you.

THE WRITING LIFE

The author wakes up, grabs her phone, and checks her email. It's Saturday. She drinks three cups of coffee and talks about them on Facebook before posting two pictures of her cats. Then she checks her email again. Two weeks and no reply! Then she goes to bed, satisfied with another day full of writing.

THERAPY

Jonah had never felt this full. The butt plug stretched his rectum more than any other object he'd ever had in there. The feeling filled his chest with something that occupied the interstitial place between love and lust. He was stroking fast now, ready to explode. Then his mother, juice in hand, opened the door.

UNDER THE PILLOW

Mommy and daddy had been fighting again. They weren't around to change the channel when the bad stuff came on. Jessica sat there and watched a man use a knife on another man. It was bloody. Now she knew why she wasn't allowed to play with them. She went to the kitchen and stole one.

JUST NOT RIGHT

Xxajj looked at the creature in front of him. It bared its teeth. Xxajj hissed and the four-legged beast evaporated. He dug around in his pockets and found the last crispy slug. It was too oily and coated his mouth with unpleasantness. This planet was just not right. He turned into light and flew away.

ILLUSIONS

After a recent conversation about the importance of illusions and how crucial it is to maintain them regardless of the situation one is in, I've decided to start carrying a suicide note at all times so that if something horrible happens to me and I die instantly, it'll still look like I was in control.

MY BREAKFAST SUCKS AND
I BLAME THE ILLUMINATI

I wake up and the world still hasn't figured out that Jackie killed him.

My neighbor has a weird scar on his forearm from when he removed the alien implant.

I turn my phone on and know that satellites secretly activate my camera and spy on me.

My breakfast sucks and I blame the Illuminati.

RIDING #5

I'm on the bus. Yes, again. A tiny blind woman is screaming into her phone. There's a tweaker, talking to himself and rocking an eyepatch, sitting way too close. His stench is making my nose hairs gag. A few seats to my right, a drunk Elvis impersonator burps and giggles. This is my Tuesday afternoon.

CRYING HEART

Frankie fears darkness. It overtakes him, and then awful things happen. It used to happen every few months. Then years would go by between episodes. Then he was sure it was gone for good. Now he blinks into existence and finds Jenny's heart in his hand, crying thick drops of blood onto the beige carpet.

INFINITE HUSTLE

It's 6:14am.

Ice covers the roofs of the cars in the parking lot.

My breath is a ghost in front of my face.

I wish I could afford a warmer jacket.

A red car drives by, spewing white smoke like a tiny round dragon with emphysema.

I smile.

It's all part of the infinite hustle.

PORCELAIN SKIN

She's young and blond. Her skin is soft to the touch and makes Joe think of a porcelain doll. Her silence is less aggressive than the silence he gets from most women. Her eyes hold no judgment. Yes, they will make love soon. Joe winks at her and slides her back into the cold chamber.

RIDING #1

There's a homeless man touching himself while he gently sobs into his filthy coat. A fat lady holds her purse close to her and looks at everyone on the bus with derision. A crazy Asian lady whispers to a tiny plant she's carrying. A transvestite dances clumsily near me. Everything is right with the world.

HYPERREALITY

Jean Baudrillard taught me that everything is a copy; nothing's original.

Jean Baudrillard taught me that everything is a copy; nothing's original.

Jean Baudrillard taught me that everything is a copy; nothing's original.

Jean Baudrillard taught me that everything is a copy; nothing's original.

Jean Baudrillard taught me that everything is a copy; nothing's original.

FRAME 313

It's usually at night. I get online and look at pictures of frame 313 of the Zapruder film. I'm a gorehound, but that's not why I do it. That blurry pink explosion isn't all that gory. No, I do it because I like to look at the exact moment this fucking nation lost its innocence.

THE BIRTHDAY PARTY

Grampa hears his daughter tell her husband they'll leave as soon as they sing Happy Birthday. Bitch didn't even make the cake. Bought one at the store. Talk about love. The kids are running around, saying he smells. Little turds don't know the difference between deaf and mute. Grampa blows the candles, wishing for death.

BLIND

Jenny wakes up. She thinks her eyes are open, but there's pain and no light. She's on a sofa, not her bed. She panics. Her right hand touches her right eye. There's only a hole there, crusty and painful. Then she remembers the hot spoon, the fear, the creatures outside. She won't see them now.

LOUD AND YOUNG AND HAPPY AND FREE

We're doing 45 on a borrowed piece of blue junk with no A/C, no radio, no brakes. The thing won't go faster. My right hand is holding the open door. My left hand is wrapped around a cheap bottle of rum. My face inches from the asphalt. We're loud and young and happy and free.

AT LEAST

The man sports a long, unkempt beard. He reeks of old sweat. No one wants to sit near him. He calls a stop. The door opens. He steps out into the rain, scratches his eyes, stands there. I look at him through the window. He's drooling. I think, "Hey, at least I'm not that guy."

THE BEGINNING OF THE END

It was a regular Tuesday. People went to work, walked their dogs, went for a jog, took the kids to the park, hated their jobs. But then things changed. All across the world, the worms started coming out of the earth. The time had come, and they were going to retake what was rightfully theirs.

MURDERED DREAMS

The skinny man stares out of his motel room window. The train tracks in the distance look thin but pregnant with promise. He brings a half-exhausted cigarette to his lips and inhales, making the bright carbuncle at the tip flare for a second.

He drowned his dreams in the variegated puddles in the parking lot.

SODA

"You'd have to kill me to get me to stop drinking soda!"

Bert said that at least twice a day. He and Sarah had been together seventeen years. Sarah did the math. She'd heard it at least 12,410 times. She was so tired, the next time he said it, she shot him in the face.

CYMOTHOA EXIGUA

Tim woke up with a hangover and couldn't feel his tongue. The appendage refused to move when he tried to lick his lips. Then something kicked against his palate. He ran to the bathroom. The last thing he expected to see when he opened his mouth was two tiny black eyes looking back at him.

TALKTALKTALK

I want to talk about how easily we travel between burning desire and ennui. I want to talk about how authors put words together in ways that destroy me and then reconstruct me. I want to talk about space, infinity, nothingness, and John Coltrane's *Interstellar Space*. Sadly, people mostly want to talk about the weather.

THE DEVIL'S DANDRUFF

Johnny the gorilla adjusted his suit and looked at Fred. The elephant sat across from him behind a mahogany desk that must've taken three sequoias to build. Fred's trunk hovered above a two-kilo mound of blow. With one powerful snort, the mountain of the devil's dandruff disappeared. Fred let out a small scream and smiled.

ALLITERATION ANNIHILATION

Bobby was a big, bad, blubbery bully who liked to bully Billy, a bashful boy who loved books. Bobby, who was all balls and no brains, bullied Billy like a bastard bozo and bothered and belittled the boy until he broke down. Then Billy brought a big black bazooka to school and blew up Bobby.

TRUTHS

Some toddlers looks like fucking junkies.

Sometimes a cleavage will generate a gravitational pull.

Folks who possess a weak handshake are worthless human beings.

Beauties usually kill beasts.

Discourse is a very dangerous thing.

Hugs can heal your soul.

Animals are better than people.

Love is a perishable thing.

We all have an expiration date.

MAKE IT STOP, DOGGIE,
I HATE MY IN-LAWS!

They had the fattest pit bull ever and locked him in a room. I wanted that monster to come barreling out and eat my face so I wouldn't have to look at them anymore. I wanted my screams to drown out the conversation. I wanted the dog to eat my heart so everything would stop.

THEY ASKED

They called him loser, fatso, and faggot. They asked him if he liked sucking horses' cocks. They asked if he jerked off to his obese dad in the shower. They asked if he borrowed his dead mom's dildo. Then he got them in the basement, and they asked him to stop, to please, please stop.

WALKING ON THE MOON

The man was bent like a discarded doll and walked with the grace of a newborn giraffe. I looked at his shoes. The heels had big springs in them.

"Hey, man, what's up with those funky shoes?" I asked.

"My back's all fucked," he said. "But don't worry, baby, 'cuz I'm walking on the moon!"

WANT/NEED

I want a car, a dog, and a house. I want money to travel, drink good booze, and smoke good shit. I want a secretary and a robot. I want to stop time and the ability to fly. I want to kill men with one punch. Thankfully, the only thing I really need is you.

JUST DON'T

Flowers the size of cars float in the air and, instead of a flowery fragrance, expel beautiful melodies into the sweet-tasting air. You glide around effortlessly and feel nothing but love. Time is irrelevant. Death is only the ghost of a bad memory. Pain is nonexistent. Now do the right thing and don't wake up.

THE ITCH

"It itches, mommy!" Betty started saying it around noon yesterday. She kept repeating it, but Sandra checked her scalp and found nothing. When Betty cried, they applied calamine. Now Sandra scratches her leg and watches Betty's bloody fingers scratch and scratch as the cerebrospinal fluid leaks from the ragged hole she's opened in her skull.

A BRIDGE MADE OF SHADOWS

Their love was a leaf in brackish water in the darkest corner of an alley where people had been stabbed.

Their love was a drop of rain coming down on a pile of skeletal corpses near a concentration camp.

Their love was a bridge made of shadows that rattled under the hooves of wild beasts.

JUST A BITE

He looked down at his arm. He felt nothing. The festering wound didn't hurt anymore. That was a good thing. It meant he couldn't feel the maggots feasting on his rotting flesh. Eight endless days in this hole and counting. Help would come. He had to stay alive. He bent down and took a bite.

BEFORE THE LAST AIRPLANE

Everyone kissed, hugged, and joked about getting hammered when they got together again. A few shared secretive looks with people they considered closer than the rest. Then some went back home and some climbed on a plane.

Only those who went home remembered what they'd done before the last plane after the place went down.

WORDS

She works with words all day. Then she goes home and writes words for a few hours. When she goes to bed, it's always with a book full of words. Unfortunately, when her husband asks if she wants water, she has to use her head to answer because no words have ever left her mouth.

GROCERY LIST

Toilet paper. American cheese. Some honesty. Bananas. A pill to forget the night she died screaming inside her burning car. Cookies. Aspirin. Sliced bread. Chicken breasts. Morphine. A promise. Something to take back what he said. A good poem. Three gods. Weed. Cider. Water to wash the sins away. Amnesia. Half a pound of youth.

NEVER

"Oh, baby, I'm sorry," said Glen. "Come on, princess, say something. You know I wouldn't hurt you."

But she said nothing.

She was done with him and done with life and done with bleeding.

Then she wasn't.

Hate brought her back, gave her new strength.

"You're not sorry, Glen, but you will be," she said.

THE BOOK CASTLE

She had a copy of Thomas Mann's *The Magic Mountain* under her arm. He was reading a book of Pablo Neruda's poetry. Their eyes met. Magic happened. They would get together and build a book castle in a remote wooded area in a beautiful mountain and live away from the rough fingers of the world.

FRIED NECKBONES

Get me some of them fine fried neckbones, man. That's where all the flavor goes. Hah! You don't even know, man. Fried neckbones and some home fries is what I'm talkin' 'bout! If you ain't never had no neckbones, you haven't lived. I'm telling you. What? Whaddaya mean this a pizza joint? Fuck you, motherfucka!

NO LONGER AT HOME

Ter-Ra-ZoN opened his seven eyes and looked at the being in front on him, a bulbous, semi-translucent thing that emitted a sound like wind through a tunnel. The air around him was bluish and so thick he could feel it going in and out of his body. He knew he was no longer at home.

CONVERSATION BETWEEN TWO MEN AT THE BUS STOP ON A MONDAY MORNING

"Found a midget living in my beard yesterday, Fred. Can't have that. Dude wasn't even paying no rent."

"Pigeons like sandwiches. Airport."

"I hear that. Last sandwich I had was bread on bread. Sad stuff."

"Kill the cowclowncone. Shave the other baby. Nuts and tricycles in Tahiti."

"I think this damn bus is running late..."

THE MUSTACHE

Roberto's mustache left him at night. It went on adventures it never talked about, but Roberto knew. Some mornings there was stuff in it that hinted at crazy things. Blood. Blow. Glitter. Green paint that one time. Roberto caressed it every morning and smiled. All was good as long as it came back to him.

FLY AWAY

Tommy could fly. He never told anyone because he felt different and knew society would treat him like a freak. Then someone caught him landing near his car at night on a phone camera and the thing went viral. In response, Tommy flew away. He was going to put that Icarus thing to the test.

SHARING

My fingers turn into snakes every night between midnight and 3:17am. My sweat makes goats horny. When I vomit, reptiles within a 5-mile radius remember a time before being born. I love the blues and it loves me back. I'm sharing these facts with you because I like you. Ignore them at your own peril.

SOME DAYS

Jenny woke up with a dead cat stuck in her throat. She went to the bathroom and the penguins that lived there shanked her in her right calf with a rusty nail. They wanted more booze and cigarettes. Then the toilet started singing opera and crying. "Well," she thought, "some days are weirder than others."

AWESOME THINGS

Some things are really awesome. Books, tacos, beer, friends, music, and mountains all fall into that category. So do smiling babies, talking parrots, nakedness, angry poets, and dogs. Also kissing, hugging, bad movies, good memories, moms, and apple juice. However, one of the awesomest things in the world is that you're reading this right now.

I REMAIN
(BACK UP OFF ME, RICKY!)

Aleathia Drehmer

I
IN SICKNESS, IN HEALTH

YOUTH FINDS A WAY OF ESCAPING

She marvels at *The Caine Mutiny* doorstop and the finger-painted wall hangings her daughter crafted years ago when innocence didn't seem like a commodity. Her eyes settle in on the reflection of her face in the glasses perched on the table. She understands for a second that life is transparent while pretending to be solid.

She was half-sleeping, trying to ignore it was 32°.

"I'm going to birth a turd," he said.

"Not in bed, I hope."

Silence... then a fart.

"You farted on me!"

"No, I farted down."

He lifted the blanket slightly.

"I don't want your damn partial Dutch Oven!"

He smiled. "I call THAT a Norwegian Toaster."

BOURBON ON THE ROCKS

The splicing of voices hovered in between the clinking of forks, and knives on pristine white dinner plates danced with the sound of water glasses being refilled and ice shifting in on new tide levels. He sat there in the silence, comparatively, with only the sound of his breathing contributing to the symphony of noise.

ESTRANGED

Her father sat at the table smoking non-filtered cigarettes and drinking coffee. He was engrossed in the morning paper and didn't look up from it when she sat in the folding chair. The blue metal was the coldest thing she had felt since coming South besides the gaping silent cavern between her and her father.

DEMEANOR

The books spoke of ladybugs bringing the languid omen of love. Bitta acted on that missive years ago and knew it was something to steer away from. It was meant to dupe her as it had last time. It was cynical laughter; her mother's cold, harsh voice in her mind whispering, "I told you so."

ANOTHER FAILURE TO
FIND CLOSURE

In a dream, my mother appeared. She looked as she had before her death. In sleep, I could feel my heart seize. We sat at the kitchen table having coffee and laughing about life moving forward. The question burning inside me never found its way from my mouth. In a moment, she was gone, again.

THIRD EYE BLIND

The keys jangled loudly in the silence between them and for a moment, she held her breath. Royce stood there helpless in his guilt, continually asking her to soil the hem of her existence, for not making an honest woman of her. Isabella thought him stupid for an augur. He should have seen this coming.

DEFEAT

Pablo wanted to paint her mouth shut and not have to listen to the thrill in her voice that signaled defeat, nor the knowing lilt that stated the quantified margins of their relationship. He understood his addiction to her body could not be overcome now that the paint flowed heavily and often in her presence.

THE CHERRY TREE

The wind came again, harder this time, shaking the cherry tree with unmitigated violence, its bare branches like nails against a chalkboard, and he was gone. Tosha froze in her disbelief, in her unwillingness to let go, in her cold and selfish grief, remembering how a smile changed everything that ever was or will be.

THE CHALLENGES OF SPACE

"I love it when you abandon me in the silence of this apartment with invisible songs and snoring cats," she muttered, "You leave me to deal with the sounds of my life alone."

"It's perfect, you know? That charged feeling pushing you to the brink. You just have to hold onto it a little longer."

BROKEN CYCLES

Lila settled for something lazy and domestic and definitely less than what she wanted. Time whispered in her delicate ear that she just wasn't worth the poetry and roses—that she should just take whomever would have her the longest. Her life became a series of stalemates and passionless loving and fights about petty things.

II
SELF-FULFILLING PROPHECIES

FORGETTABLE

I have always straddled the line, hitched my skirt up at the edge of these two worlds I was born into.

None of them want me, black or white, don't see how my mixed up body gives them blessing to love and hate without remorse. I could give them treasures if they'd only look beneath.

ON THE FIX

She heard the crack vial crush under her sandal. The grinding glass felt like a torture that ran up her leg, lodged into her throat. She wished she weren't so high. She wished she could stand up from the condom strewn bench and scream. She could only sit there among secretions of strangers, crying silently.

THE SCAR

On her face lies a deep scar, irreverent and penetrating. It's unable to be wished away with hope; unable to be patched by love into a wholeness, which she longs for. It will always keep her from truth. It will always keep her in the arms of pity, but never in the arms of sympathy.

THE ORIGINAL ME

I do this because it all hurts too much. I'm drowning in false realities bred from the loins of my fantasy. In the end, I am wet and outdated. There is no way to return to the original me, to know who that ever was. It tells me what I have erased from your tongue.

FEEDBACK

The feedback stayed with Jean ever since Fred smashed his guitar against the wall. It shrieked and vibrated against her membrane and made her nauseous. The ringing made the world seem intolerable with her eyes open. Using more than one sense at the same time pushed too close to the line of being insanely overboard.

ILLEGAL ALIEN

The summer calm before the rains came brought Marquessa much grief. She did not remember being so uncomfortable in the heat of the desert; only now in the lush green of the flats of Iowa did she suffer the moist, shocking weather. It felt like a million moray eels suffocating her bones in a coil.

2am INEPTITUDE

Awkwardly, Di held her dead hand trying to slide off the wedding rings. Her skin, like cold clay, gave resistance. The gold circle spun, a large document, uploading. She looked away with sudden 2am ineptitude. His warm fingers were a rescue. I put them on, he said, I'll be the one to take them off.

SYMPHONY NOT SYMPATHY

Downstairs, the dog is having a seizure on the tile. His whimpering cries rising from the depths of his guts, his paws scraping ceramic run in time to the tapping of keys beneath my frozen fingers. Part of me thinks I should sit close and comfort him, but I don't have it in me to.

DISGUST

She noted the upswept hair, dull in color; dry as straw except for the parts greasy from not washing. She looked with disgust at the breasts hanging there like beggars waiting for their version of alms for the poor. They looked so useless in their age, the whole body standing with the inability to feel.

DREAMS OF A DRUGSTORE COWBOY

Joan caught her aging reflection in triplet in the angled mirrors of the medicine cabinet. Those women staring back at her suddenly unrecognizable—so much older and fatter than she last remembered. Her chin sagged below the jaw, the lack of sleep burgeoning from beneath her eyes. *This can't be what I've become,* she thought.

CONFESSIONS

The dried maple leaves skittered across the pavement, their points like sharpened teeth, sounding like millions of rats scurrying. She wanted them to swallow her. She wanted to disappear in a flux of wind. She begged for it like a sinner. She wanted to be reclaimed back to the earth. She wanted to stop being.

III
CONFABULATIONS

UNFINISHED TWINS

Claudine laughed hysterically as the garbling went on for an hour. It was possibly the most impossible conversation ever to occur on the planet. The women's mouths weren't fully painted. Each was left with a corner in which to try and squeak out their meaning in life. They were nothing more than paint to canvas.

BE CAREFUL WHAT YOU WISH FOR

The smaller version of himself lay there in a fitful dream. His limbs jerked and his face torqued in a supernatural expression of pain. Mark was beginning to question the lines of his own lucidity. He heard his tiny body scream out and something in him needed to comfort the tortured soul in the bed.

ABSINTHE

His head was gone, well not completely gone, more so replaced with a line drawing of the most beautiful cathedral he had ever seen. It was meticulous and grand. The stained glass windows were aglow with an abhorrent beauty. They flickered as he felt himself blink. His fingers shook with utter disbelief and true madness.

EXISTENTIAL BIRD ON A WIRE

Her body folded in half before she felt the cool, round ballast under her hand. There was no sign of the bird; no tiny feet clinging to her index finger like in the dream. She rolled her body back to its original position, leaned against the wall. She touched her finger again to find nothing.

INFECTION

He said there's a fire. I agreed. It's burning in the attic of my spleen, destroying my immunity and my ability to fight off the infection of his words. It left me hot and crazy like tropical disease. We spoke of infernos—some real, some imagined, while the Girl from Ipanema roamed in my head.

UNILATERAL SUMMATIONS

Georgia made calculations on the steamed windows of the shower, the hot water scalding her flesh. Her body claimed it was late, her mind said early, so she scratched equations into the surface of water molecules to prove they were both wrong. One controlled the other, guiding the summation unilaterally. The war would never end.

SPY

I am invisible or maybe I'm in this rock and I am really a microphone-wiretap-bug. I can't be sure of anything other than the fact that I feel paranoid. I am trying to listen to his conversations. I put a glass up to my ear, but I don't have a wall to press it to.

OBSESSIONS

Barb walked through the reference section in the library. Each step metered like poetry to the syllables of the word "desiccated". One, two, three, four counted the other half of her brain; steps and letters and steps and letters. Her body moved with primal focus, thinking of footfalls and strewn guts of animals in hot sun.

THE BAPTISM

He took her hand this time. He liked the softness of it, so he held it awhile. They said nothing. He put his good energy into that hand resting lightly in his. He felt Marnie's body gradually slacken the longer he held it. He felt her mood soften some. It was time for the water.

IF THE KEY FITS

The key only fit halfway through the lock, felt like it would break, and not be removed.

Fuckfuckfuckfuckfuckfuckfuckfuck.

She tried the other doors: more of the same. At the hatchback she prepared herself for the usual dance. Open hatch, crawl through, fall into the seat, kick the door furiously... swearing.

Winter is officially fucking here.

THE REINCARNATION OF THE BATTLE OF THE BABYLONIANS AND THE GREEKS FOR INTELLECTUAL SUPREMACY

"Talking is options," said the shower stall. "Mathematic calculations are not."

"I don't want to hear one word from you until you figure out the square root of the water droplets on the five walls."

"Bu..."

"I SAID NO TALKING!!!" screamed the shower.

"128.26534995585917," she smiled.

"GOD DAMN IT! You always guess 16,452."

"I win."

IV
FACE DOWN, ASS UP

QUEEN OF THE BEES

Darla closed her eyes and swam through the honey pit, arms moving in slow motion and legs scissoring, but not cutting anything but time. Her naked flesh invited the honey to live on her. She opened her mouth and tasted it. It was so sweet and natural that it choked her. It transcended everything unnamable.

A WET DREAM

The teenage clerk watched in amazement as she brought her clenched fist towards her mouth and placed the entire hand inside of it. Her elbow quivered in the air as she rooted around inside her throat for something large. The clerk noted how she did not gag. She struggled with the contents in her mouth.

JAZZ HANDS

A man once told me I had bravado. I wasn't sure what that meant so I kept on kissing him like I meant it. He told me my tongue was magic as I took him in my mouth and all I could think about were top hats and white gloves as he spilled over me.

SILENT SADIST

He looked deep and long into the melancholy, writing a symphony across her face. He worked patiently and gently to remove the tape. It left a tacky, wet feeling against her pale ankles and he ran his fingers over it. Phoebe's eyes glimmered momentarily and one side of her mouth curled upward ever so slightly.

SAMPSON AND DELILAH

His mouth was fierce against mine, his tongue jagged with desire against the soft insides of my mouth. His hands gripped into my back while I stood there not reciprocating, but not rejecting either. His hands ran over my buttocks and pulled me closer in a demanding way. I felt myself soften at his hunger.

GAME OF FLESH

They grabbed at her like rude men on a city street; cat called her, trying to rip pieces of flesh from her bones. She swatted at them. Marilla felt them laughing as she missed her mark more often than not. They laughed at her, because she could not see them and she became their game.

PRESUMED TORTURE

Her hair plastered to her forehead, moans muffled when he tightened the gag ball between her lips, leaving her without any mercy or retribution. He recited shitty poetry from memory, each line ended on a thrust that pulled her guts out through her pussy with no regret, breaking any will she had left to fight.

FORGIVE ME FATHER

Her tongue is a salt flat left when the sun has taken away what she loves the most. She senses her hand in Father Amis' hand, and it gives her a deep, uneasy feeling of connectedness that she does not desire, and in his skin, she can feel the evil no one else can see.

DARK NINJA SEX

His howls sailed through the air like dark ninja sex, full of knives and bleeding and deadly stars in eyes. It vibrated the windows and her bones until she could feel the calcium leaking from her marrow in a grand, suffocating exit fit for Scarlett O'Hara on her worst day. There was no escaping him.

LAST MEMORY

He'd never know her like that. Not as some flesh bound mystery. Not as a rainstorm inside a glass. Not as simplicity. It would always be this moment held at arm's length, and it would always hurt like a last kiss. He would go back into her quiet place, always waiting for the sirens, waiting.

A WOMAN'S PLACE

The smell of the Comet went to her head and Sandy realized she had been on her knees a long time scrubbing the same spot in the tub that was now beautiful and clean under the streaks of green-blue grit. The bathroom rug meshed into her flesh so deeply that it didn't hurt any longer.

V
THE EVIL IN ALL OF US

WELCOME TO BEDLAM

Her naked body was twisted and old as they held her down on dishwater gray sheets. There was devil in that woman's eyes Maria never wanted to see again. The nurse pierced her from over her shoulder with a syringe clenched between her teeth. Maria step backwards. She let the door close in her face.

THE DEVIL

He tells him to quit scratching at the door like a Vietnamese prostitute. He looks down on the pitiful remnants of this man, places his boot on his fingers, relishing in the sound of joints popping and bones breaking. He spits on him.

"Get out of my way, you fucking scum, you make me sick."

PANIC

At the edge of the tree line, she stood hunched over with her hands on her knees, chest heaving for air. Her mind went completely numb after finding Jackson with blood on his hands, standing at the sink frantically scrubbing. She noticed a look of insanity on his face and how he smelled of panic.

BONES OF A FRIEND

The bones feel disconnected in his hands; they feel limp like a sleeping infant. Barnabus is almost afraid to peel back the silken edges, afraid of what he might find, though the linear part of his brain knows very well what he will see. They gleam against the blanket, against the succulent soil in mounds.

THE HORDE

They ganged up on her dressed as clowns from her nightmares; demons of her sleep. They cackled in her ears, smearing white and red face paint across her cheeks and in her hair. She could smell the decay of their collective mouths. The sight of their noses encircling her sent her into a violent seizure.

AB-

His face streaked with trails his fingers made as he painted himself in AB- from the local Red Cross. Eltsen wondered which housewife from his town was sitting on his lips, in his hair, and gluing his eyelashes together. He tasted her on his tongue, wished it was real... wished her flesh between his teeth.

REPEATING MISERY

He wondered if his neck was broken and maybe he couldn't get up or if he was just sick to death of repeating his miseries. He lay there breathing in the disrespect of other men, men just like him and thought, considering his actions in life, this was as good a penance as any other.

PINK FLAMINGOS

Thomas started swinging. The sound of plastic on plastic was new music to his ears. The sound of flamingo heads exploding on contact, the sound of shrapnel like from the war, edged him further. He went right down the line beheading those damn gay pink birds. He couldn't stop. He felt addicted to that sound.

DEATH COMES TOO QUICK

The sound of the cane on the hardwood floors makes a hollow thumping compared to the scratching shuffle of her moccasins; each step moving her outside the lighted circle, each step growing colder and heavier in her lungs. Sally stands at the window, her breath fogging the panes, and watches the darkness take over everything.

THE ROOT OF EVIL IS CLOSER THAN YOU THINK

She couldn't look away, and all that was good riled inside her. Ingrid felt the icy tendrils crawl over her pale winter skin; needling her vital places; strangling the essence of her heart. For the first time in her life, Ingrid understood her Lord's fair warning. She stood witness to the defamation of her soul.

JUDGMENT

Sovann stood there, mouth agape at the power he felt swimming down the stairs from the temple. He was afraid. He did not want to open the door to his soul. He did not want to hear Boupha calling him with the tendrils of the trees, with rain drops, with the sweat of his body.

CORE WORLDS

Matthew Revert

CONSIDER THIS THAT

I wish I had written something to place in your pocket before you were burned. Perhaps nothing more than an introduction to a careful stranger, but one who cherished you deeply. I am grateful I pressed my lips against you, even though I swore I would not. I remembered the warmth you no longer possessed.

NIGHTLIGHT

The plumber turns on the nightlight so the pipes may sleep without their usual fear.

"Did you do it?" asks the plumber's wife.

"I did."

He struggles into bed and pulls the blankets to his chin. His wife turns off the bedside lamp. The plumber lies afraid in the dark, wishing he had his nightlight.

BENCH

I saw your face in the purple bruise I placed on my knee. I was given the bruise by a steel bench that no longer needed it. I took the bruise before I knew your face lived within, and when I discovered you there, I did all I could to convince the bruise to stay.

BYE, CHILD

He was so surprised at the sight of 10,000 moths stealing his son that he never thought to prevent it.

"Where's Joey?"

"You're not going to believe this. Moths took him."

"Why didn't you stop them?"

"It didn't occur to me."

They stared into the distance, wondering if it was appropriate to mention dinner plans.

...AND GIVES THE BOOK TO HIS WIFE

Clouds glance down to see what shapes we form.

A young couple sits at a café sharing a milkshake.

It is always another late afternoon.

A bus has broken down and the passengers have been asked to disembark.

A child tries to escape his shadow.

An elderly man finds a book left in a park.

LOST YOUTH

As a child I was given the opportunity to ride a walrus to school, but turned this opportunity down. Each morning, fellow students would pass me by on their walruses, and they always looked so full of joy. I tried to correct this regret by riding a walrus to work, but it wasn't the same.

ATTEMPTED COUPLE

Their first date was in a sewer.
She had mutton.
He had damper.
They kissed and their breath tangled like poorly cast fishing line.
Their final date was their second.
It was in the same sewer.
She didn't eat.
He had mutton.
They thought about kissing one another goodbye, but decided they preferred uninterrupted breath.

SHADOW MAN

It was a valiant attempt to beat *Mega Man 3*, but once again, he died at Shadow Man. He had studied the proposed order one should beat the bosses in, but even so, his abilities were lacking. This is why his wife left. She was married next month to someone who could beat Shadow Man.

MISTAKEN FISHERMAN

He called himself a fisherman, yet there was nothing to substantiate this claim. He owned no fishing apparatus and had never been fishing, yet if you engaged him in conversation, "I am a fisherman," was the first thing he said. When asked why, he would stare romantically into the distance as though surveying the ocean.

CROHNS

He was bleeding from the inside, so nobody knew. Without a single rivulet for the skin to wear, one can still don a nice suit and attend a polite dinner. It's amazing what the body hides. He could spend the whole night with you, and you wouldn't even know how badly he was falling apart.

RIVERBANK

Set your heart aglow then place it in a lantern. Send it down the river to nod at the night. Be kind to the children who congregate at the riverbank. They came for water but have become absorbed by the subtle illumination you give to the sky. Every beat gives breath to the gentle light.

THANK YOU

Everyone else is asleep. He makes his children sandwiches with stale bread, wishing his day were ending rather than beginning. The bread breaks as the peanut butter is spread. He says a silent apology to his sleeping children, wishing he could provide something that pleased their stomachs while filling it. He leaves silently for work.

HENRY'S NOSE

"Your snoring is TERRIBLE, Henry."

"Don't blame me! I gotta passenger in me nose."

"What are you on about, ya sod?"

"A passenger! A nose traveller. He's a loud bastard, he is."

"Ask him to leave then!"

"I can't do that. It wouldn't be right."

"Why the devil not?"

"Coz he's me son, ain't he."

COGNITIVE INTERCEPTION

There should be a place where my words and actions go to receive an assessment before they are permitted into the world. It is tiring to say or do the wrong thing with such consistent expertise. I am prepared to wait if it minimises damage. When my pen dies, I should not seek out another.

BODY OIL

They purchased refurbished veins to carry their body oil into gunk chambers, where it was collected by thirsty starling beaks and regurgitated into the stomachs of their young.

"You cannot cook with the oil, but you can cook the oil."

Starlings cannot understand such instruction, but they never cook with the oil inside us anyway.

CARTWHEELS

Inside every boredom lives an absolute pleasure of existence wishing you would embrace it. Dislodge yourself with cartwheels in gardens. You still move forward like a flower drinking sunlight. Your worst day is similar to every other, but you ignore this in favor of petty despairs. Your happiness exists and deserves to know you care.

HOME VIDEOS

A family is gathered around home videos of an unknown family. These strangers perform for the camera, becoming the momentary family everyone sees in the restless light behind eyes forced shut by summer.

"Be them," says the father to his children, pointing at the screen.

The children scrunch shut their eyes and move into position.

ALLOWANCE

The equation has been modified to include her, but does not allow for fluctuation. She must remain the uneasy silence between hum and buzz so the equation maintains its answer. He hoped she could sustain on the pause between words when one reloads their breath. She lasted as long as she could before walking away.

HAPPY NEW YEAR

Have you ever undressed for a doctor when you didn't think it was necessary? Was a prognosis formed based on your frail nudity shrinking before the doctor's eyes? Were you touched only where it hurt? Were you happy to be charged for the consultation? Did you go home afterward and spend New Year's Eve ashamed?

SPLINTS

One of her splints is in Brooklyn and should be there tomorrow. The other is in Arizona. I am writing a letter to her father warning him of impending war. I was asked not to do this before the splints arrived. War, like a child, only pretends to wait. Why suppose the opposite is true?

LACK OF CHINA

Teacher asked her students to make origami chimney-sweeps but didn't give them paper. When the students sat confused, doing nothing, teacher got angry and kicked a model globe of the world.

"Didn't have China on it anyway."

At the back of class, despite having no paper, one student completed her origami chimney-sweep and said nothing.

NAIVETY

I want you to feel the least amount of unhappiness you are capable of feeling. There's no energy left to care about anything else except for my cat. It's hard to be scared of waking up, or wondering if it's wrong to sleep. I listen to the blackbird in my garden fight its reflection again.

SHARED INCUBATION

Our genesis can be traced back through the reproductive organs of swans. Or a swinging string of saliva on a drunken bottom lip. There could be a topiary maze we get lost in. I could pretend I know the constellations and point them out to you. We should try being us without consequence more often.

PENGUIN

The kids threw their hat in the big crock-pot so their mother could boil all the germs out. Jimmy drew a penguin on his tummy at lunchtime, which his mother asked him to wash off before dinner.

"Don't want to."

"Why not?"

"Don't want to kill the penguin."

"You'd better feed it every day then."

REASONS I WOULDN'T LIKE
LIVING UNDER THE SEA

1. Very wet
2. Need for oxygen
3. Poor Wi-Fi connectivity
4. Have never liked seafood
5. My stools would float
6. Intimidated by lampreys
7. Prone to serious ear infections
8. Underwater photographers
9. Likely wouldn't fit inside a clam shell
10. Fishermen mythologizing me
11. *Dawson's Creek* DVDs wouldn't work
12. No onions

TRAINS

On a crowded train, people often forget to suppress their all-encompassing sadness. It can be seen in the plaintive stares out dirty windows, or the moment one glances away from their book. Perhaps the train's movement recreates private moments, forcing us inward to regard the everyday miseries inside us. Forgetting perceived scrutiny is genuine freedom.

BOARD GAME EVENT

Mum cooking casserole again. The house smells like an abattoir farted. Dad swims through the cauliflower steam and rescues trapped water. I had to invent a board game at school today, but I forgot to invent the instructions. My brother and I play while the casserole birds escape their flatulent stench, splashing into my wall.

TURNS OUT IT WASN'T *SCUM*

I have been trying to load a website purporting to list Napalm Death's albums from worst to best. For whatever reason, the page refuses to load, no matter how long I let it sit. All I can tell you is *Harmony's Corruption* is listed as their worst. I suspect *Scum* is touted as their best.

CAKE MAN

Never disturb the man in the cake. I know it's your birthday and you are enticed by the icing, but if you cut this cake, you will kill the man inside. He wasn't baked inside. He grew from bacteria formed in the air pockets. If you hold your ear against it, you'll hear him breathing.

ABSORBING STORIES

It is okay to give the occasional night to your sadness, but understand, the more nights you give, the less they start to give back. A wall can only absorb so much before it no longer has stories to capture. That cobweb the cornice wears has been empty longer than your sadness has been full.

SANS AMPLIFY

Grace sat cross-legged, piercing her thigh with fork tines. It lowered the world's volume enough to hear what whispered below the squawk. Should I respond to my skin when it speaks? The skin's *yes* sounds like the hissing of snakes falling from statues. Grace looked at her thigh holes and inhaled the smoke curling out.

WHAT WOULD YOU LIKE TO DO?

I knew a woman who married the paperclip that offered assistance in early versions of Microsoft Word. He was, on the surface, as helpful as one would expect and the early days of their marriage were rewarding. At first, her new husband helped with basic formatting issues, but eventually all possible assistance scripts were exhausted.

WATCHMEN

He was hired to prop open the eyes of tired watchmen. A finger here. Another there. Eyelids were prevented from meeting, as though depriving the coming together of soul mates.

"What are you watching for?" he asked one day.

"Something better."

He directed his gaze as they did and saw the uneasy calm before violence.

CIVIC RESPONSIBILITY

In the sleeplessness, which clambers upon the skin of night, I hear a crash outside my window. Two cars coming together in a new gnarl of burnt shapes.

Then screaming.

One woman alone amid chaos I cannot see from the warmth of my sleepless bed.

Hours pass. The screaming remains. Why will nobody help her?

POSSIBLE URINE

I have eight two-liter bottles beside my bed filled with varying amounts of urine. This may or may not be true. When in bed, the notion of making a premature exit for any reason strikes me as anathema. I can assure you, this second statement is true, but I shall not commit to the first.

CHANGE

“You look different to how I remember.”
“I’ve changed. “
“Impossible.”
“Why?”
“People cannot change. The bounds of their being are formed early.”
“I disagree. I have changed the color of every cell.”
“Paint a black wall white, it is still the same wall.”
“Perhaps your perception is stunted.”
“I know for a fact it is.”

DELAYED GRATITUDE

"Thank you."

"Why are you thanking me?"

"You gave me a bite of your sandwich thirty years ago and I never said thanks."

"It was nothing. You don't have to thank me."

"It was a good gesture which deserved recognition."

"Thing is, you DID thank me back then."

"Really?"

"Yes."

"Disregard everything I just said."

MISSING CHILD

The child was last seen retrieving an ostrich egg from the chimney.

"Get in there," said his father. "You're small enough."

The child obeyed and scaled the house, arriving at the chimney and shimmying inside. The father giggled a silly giggle before galloping home. The egg fried in the pan. He wouldn't have to share.

CHAPERONE

Slide a wee mirror in your skin so your veins can do their hair. There's a dance coming up and they've been practicing their dabke. Give them a plate of herring and watch them slurp and suck like alley cats who believe every meal is their last. You'll reminisce about this one day and smile.

BAKER'S DOUGH

They got drunk on the rooftop together and watched the bakers down below bicker with their dough.

"You can really taste the pear in this cider."

"Pipe down a moment. Look at that."

One baker had reconciled with his dough and apologized for all the pain he had caused.

"I think they're going to kiss."

EAR

The child lies awake in bed at 4:30am, listening to his mother scream from the shower. The water is scalding and she must endure it until her husband can lessen the heat.

The child lies awake in bed at 5:00am, listening to his mother crying in pain from the earlier shower. His father is apologizing.

STAMINA

I once wore an old skirt and danced for my mother to distract her from the illness taking over her body. She laughed until there were tears and I did the same. What a perfect distraction it was, but of course I could not dance forever, even though part of me was prepared to try.

THE SURGEON IS DYING

He was the last surgeon left in the world and he needed a heart operation. The queues of people requiring surgical assistance stretched from his door like arms in the morning. His heart beat with lessening confidence, moving toward total failure. He numbed his chest before sliding the scalpel inside, but still felt unbearable pain.

PURPOSE

I could, in a gentle moment, embrace my ancillary purpose, becoming your whimsical Australian logophile and imaging fields for us to roll around in. Firing periods toward your sentences, allowing them to end gracefully, dutifully. Pulling your paragraphs down like blinds so only the wings of passing traffic light can understand the room we share.

CONSUMER DATA

I continue taking a Buzzfeed quiz regarding which day of the week I am until I become anything other than Tuesday. The hopelessness of Tuesday is the resignation of Monday replaced by the despair Monday imbued. It is a fitting day for a funeral, reminding those in attendance Tuesday will not continue looming torment forever.

SUITABLE FOR DAILY USE

We met in a shampoo commercial. I was before and you were after. You were the result of my splits finding repair.

Perfect ends.

The shower drain was clogged with cathode word games you inevitably won while I worked the dials. I tried to break through damaged reception to glance your drapes of TV hair.

STOMACH

He told her life was pathogenic and she pressed a quieting finger against his lips.

We will do one another harm, he thought.

The pain in his stomach called toward all other pain and the response was silence until the response was her and only her. One finger stopping the world from knowing its end.

BRICK PARANOIA

He believed someone was removing bricks from his home and replacing them with others while he slept. He spent time applying a signature to each brick in turn. He woke the next morning and set out to verify the signed bricks all remained undisturbed. It disappointed him greatly to discover no bricks possessed his signature.

THE FIRST THING I EVER READ

Sat on father's knee. We both held open the book.

"What's it called?"

"Don't know."

"Sound it out. What's the first letter?"

"M."

"Now what's the second?"

"E."

"What sound does M make?"

"Muhhh."

"And the E?"

"Eeeeee."

"Put the sounds together."

"Muhhh eeeee. Muhhheeeeee. M... muhee."

"Nearly."

"Muhee. M... Me. ME!"

"You got it!"

TABITHA

My first cat died before school.
Her name was Tabitha.
Cars ran her body in two.
We called dad at work.
He came home to remove Tabitha's halves.
At school I wanted to cry.
I told some friends about Tabitha and they laughed.
This is when I stopped believing in the possibility of good people.

THINGS WE CANNOT

Ty counted his fingers all day and never arrived at the same number. *My fingers are wrong,* he thought. When Michael arrived, it looked like he had been crying. Cello strings coiled from his eyes.

"I cannot count my fingers," said Ty.

"I cannot play my eyes," replied Michael.

They embraced like wood and fire.

CONCIERGE

A lot is expected of me, yet nothing is expected of me. I guess you have not seen me following behind, stitching shut the tears in your vapor trail. I charted your predicted path and woke up early to remove all the dead animals strewn along it. I know it upsets you to see them.

BASKETBALL STAR

On the day of my mother's funeral, my basketball team played with black bands around their arms.

"What are these for?" I asked a fellow player.

"Umm... because of your mum," he replied with discomfort.

We lost by a wide margin and I cannot recall ever having played so poorly. *For you, mum,* I thought.

FACTORY SEEDS

Mrs. McCormick gave the factory seeds away to anyone who purchased one of her teacakes. Most were forgotten in drawers or thrown away, but those that met soil sprouted their factories immediately. These were factories before computers, where men and women died trying to meet unreasonable productivity quotas. They grew without needing care or water.

WANT

I want to think of something as simple as a straw and invent it. I want to be responsible for something new that appears as though it has always been. I want to kiss someone whose lips kiss back. When knocked to the ground, I want to stay there and feel justified in doing so.

PARADISE FALLS

Grant Wamack

WHAT THE NIGHT BROUGHT IN

We had gotten wasted the night before and found ourselves in a retro-themed diner. It was still early. We were still faded, yet business seemed to be booming. I sipped my lemon water, feeling like the desert had ravaged my insides, and I stared at the waitresses' curves—the only stable thing in this oasis.

A THIEF'S TIME

It took us five hours to dig up the bastard. Shouldn't have taken so long, but the coffin was huge. We lifted the lid and the smell made us gag like amateur porn stars. My partner cut the obese body open and chunks of cotton streamed out.

"Fuck is this? Some sort of joke?"

"Nope."

DO DRUGGIES DREAM
OF STATIC LINES?

I snorted a lot in my lifetime. Cocaine, ketamine, speed, xan, mdma and a bunch of other acronyms. Great times, hazy memories. One time I snorted something called "smart dust" for a pay-check. Nano robots surged through my sinuses, embedding themselves into my system. Ten razorblades and two white lines later and they're still here.

ONLY NATURAL

Patrick was born with a cornucopia of fruit sprouting from his pelvis instead of normal genitalia. He embraced his abnormality and so did the media. He became an overnight celebrity and an advocate for non-GMO produce and an environmentalist. Still, he couldn't admit to his beautiful mistress that some of his fruit had gone bitter.

THE WORLD ON MUTE

Turquoise rocks surrounded his bony wrist and hung around his neck like sacred jewels. They told him it would open his throat chakra, give him the ability to talk for once—communicate. Lift him from the box old doctors and weak genes placed him in. He furiously rubbed the stones, willing vocal cords to blossom.

BIRD WATCHING

My girl forced me to pull over when she spotted the bird. We were an hour away from the motel, but I did as she wished. She hopped out the passenger seat and managed to catch the ruby-throated hummingbird. She forced its beak open and pulled out a string of precious stones covered in saliva.

WHALE SONGS

We fucked like animals while listening to whale songs. I know it was a strange fascination, but Sonia said it would bring us closer together, put us on the same wavelength. She loved talking about vibrations and how nothing remains motionless. When I snapped her neck, I wondered how solid her theory was, and sighed.

THESE HANDS OF MINE

Mom said I was way too handsome to be throwing hands. But my hands were big ugly things, covered in back alley tats and calluses. Made no sense that I was a model. Should've been a boxer. Pops thought different. Had to give him the hands. Stake my claim on his face. Leave my mark.

SINGAPORE EAR

Foster knew he was in trouble once he saw the stringy, cotton wool-like substance inside the woman's ear. He scooped away a mass of almond brown wax. He thought it was a minor infection, but the white webby substance twitched and a white quivering parasite crawled out the darkness, striving to feel another human's touch.

MY TYPE OF PARTY

Mira knew she was late, but took her time applying her makeup anyway. When she entered her friend's apartment, the lights were off and candles lit. Her friends wore haysacks with weird patches covering their eyes. Following suit, Mira pulled on her sensory mask, and smearing her concealer quickly became the least of her worries.

BRAIN CELLS

I burned too many brain cells to be worried about whatever's in the attic. Nonetheless, I'm still worried sick. Paranoid's more like it. Think it might be the weed. Might be laced. There it goes again. Banging. Lovers. Derelicts. Coming down. Heavy steps. Eyelids too low to make out the wavering shapes. Smells like Christmas.

EXHIBIT A

A man crouches in front of Santa Muerte. She stares down at him behind hollow eyes and a head adorned with beads and a tear-stained veil. He clasps his dirty hands and prays hard. Mentions a lost son, a sick mother... the list goes on. Shaking uncontrollably, the man stands and the candles go out.

INTIMATE MOMENTS

Listening to jazz somehow led to sex on the beach which led to staring at the stars. He woke with sand in places he forgot existed, and coughed up a wad of phlegm in the sink.

"Bloody hell."

Took a piss and shook out the remaining droplets. They sprinkled the floor like a holy christening.

SKELETONS IN THE CLOSET

The skeletons had been hoarding guns in the closet for the last decade, knowing the day would come when their owners would try to dispose of them once and for all.

The doorknob turned clockwise.

The most ancient skeleton gripped a sawed-off shotgun and chewed on a toothpick.

Sunlight swept the closet.

Gunfire. Cordite.

Liberation.

BRACE FOR IMPACT

Mom said my diet would have to change since the braces were put in. I couldn't indulge in certain cravings. Thought I could deal, but the urge welled up like a volcano and was bound to go off. That moment came prom night, and I'm still struggling to pick my date out of my teeth.

SIREN CALL

Doug leaned over the edge and wiped the bile from his lips. The ocean was black as oil, and the smell of saltwater made him nauseous.

Snippets of women singing softly. He squinted his eyes. Lithe bodies arose, revealing perky tits and alabaster skin.

The sirens compelled Doug to climb the railing and dive in.

DRESS CODE

Monday: Japanese denim jeans, Alexander Wang jacket.

Tuesday: White button-up shirt. Boring slacks.

Wednesday: Bape flip-flops. Cheetah print panties. Digital watch.

Thursday: Heart on my sleeve. White gloves so I can weep over MJ.

Friday: Five gold chains and hoop earrings.

Saturday: Sequin body dress that makes me feel like a mermaid.

Sunday: Birthday suit.

CHAMBER ROUGE

The books spewed from her heaving chest. Hardcovers, paperbacks, chapbooks, zines, graphic novels. She flipped through pages with slick hands, pouring over genetic narratives as blood pooled around her trembling legs in the dying light. When death came for her, surrounded by dust motes and red crows, she embraced him, knowing she would be back.

LINE-UP

All I wanted was a quick line-up, but there were zombies in the barbershop. Old and young men hobbling under faulty lighting. I looked down at my decaying flesh and swallowed hard. I was once told to blame it on the alcohol, but this time—this time—I blamed it on those damn bath salts.

EYE SEE

She was my dealer, but I swear she had drugs in her eyes. I could stare in them shits for hours and she would charge me for every single minute. I tried to leave and find optical tokes elsewhere. Wasn't the same. When I returned, the high intensified tenfold, and her cornea swallowed me whole.

WING IT

The woman flew down and embraced Leif in her wings. They smelled like damp caves, curry, and selenite. He kissed her neck while fingering the throbbing veins that ran across her back.

Melting down to the floor, she tightened her wings around the old man's body, shutting out the sunlight and breaking his brittle bones.

AUX CORD

"Can you pass the aux?"

Jodee trembled as she passed the cord off.

Raquel plugged the male end into the cracked mp3 player, smiled wickedly, and pressed play.

The windows blew out, shattering into a fine dust. The bass shook the car's rusted frame and Jodee's eardrums popped and her ear canals filled with blood.

PAREIDOLIA

My doctor said we all do it. See patterns in everything. Nothing to worry about, but I think he might be wrong. I saw my mom's bloated face staring at me from my soggy cereal, my uncle's lazy eye lodged inside the rings of a tree's trunk, and God's visage smeared across my neighbor's mailbox.

DAME FUEGO

The motherfucker couldn't even roll. Smooth out the hollow cigar papers, move the weed into place, and roll. He struggled to seal the blunt with his pathetic tongue. That pink wad of flesh. I grabbed my lighter and lit him up. Flailing his arms like a phoenix, I watched him learn how to truly roll.

THE PAPERCUT ARTIST

A homeless gypsy stumbled into a renowned art gallery and bumped into a painting while holding his grubby hand. Spectators cleared a space around him as he revealed his shaking index finger. He blew cold air on his prominent paper cut. The crowd whipped out their camera phones, snapping photos while others clapped in awe.

SPIN THE BOTTLE

I caught my sister vomiting out back. She wiped her mouth and looked at me like a rabid dog. Tried comforting her, but she ran away. I looked down at the black mess. Chunks of yellow floating. Swirling trails of quasars. I outstretched my arm, daring to touch it, but I only found a void.

THE COPPER TAPES

The cops beat the VHS tape to death. It lay on the floor surrounded by cigarette buds and porn.

The plastic casing containing the psychedelic-laced reels was shattered and black shiny innards were exposed. Magnetic tape spooled out in spirals and the film spores rose like dust motes.

The cops fell into coughing spurts, dying.

NO FILTER

The photographer moved the model in front of the white background.

"Take a breath. Relax. You've done this before."

"But..."

"No filters. We're going natural. You wanted this."

"Yes, but I'm not sure if they're ready."

"You agreed to no filters."

She nodded and took off her face and let it float to the floor.

RAP HANDS

Sean squatted, Gucci cape trailing, and threw up his hands. Rotating palms and a flick of the wrist. The audience stared in awe.

When Sean was put to rest, his hands were cut off and sold at an underground auction. Lucy caressed his stiff fingers, opened her legs and put the hands to good use.

INFINITE SMILES

The auditorium is packed. You stand under the spotlight and grip the mic like an old lover. First joke, delivered smooth as a jab, brings the crowd to tears. You're just warming up, but you freeze and gaze into the audience, catching open mouths and lost revelations. A panorama of smiles infinite, white and gleaming.

MODERN RUINS

Ricardo peeled his face back like a banana peel and gently folded the weathered skin. A green motherboard whirred inside the contours of his face and lights flashed on and off. He fiddled with the central processing unit and something hissed. His mouth opened. "Death is but a circuit board humming away into the night."

COSMOLOGICAL FANGS

A group of men and women buckled themselves in. They were being sent into space to investigate a coffin-like object on Mars. Gabriela prayed the shuttle would explode, while Henry wondered if getting bit would be so bad. Michael wished he did another line of coke before the launch. The high was already wearing off.

RED WINGS

"Are you ready to earn your wings?"

"What?"

Roxee shoved Nate's face into her wet pussy and his mouth was engulfed by pink folds of labia. He felt like he was being stuffed into a fleshy origami piece and began exploring the angles with his tongue.

He tasted copper and stopped.

Roxee laughed.

"Congrats, darling."

BROKE BACK NATION

My momma died last summer. They said she had a broken back. Doctor claimed her withered spine cracked like a twig under pressure. I threw my boots out, overwhelmed with guilt. A month later, I took some cement and repaired that crack in the sidewalk. Momma's back, but she still reeks of earth and decay.

THE CHALK DUST SCRIPTURES

The boy was forced into the schoolyard. He held two black erasers and smashed them together, imagining his teacher's chubby face lodged in between. Clouds of chalk dust engulfed the child. He coughed until his vision turned white and the sky spun thick webs. Spiders crawled out the cracks and taught him a new religion.

FA$HION MANIA

The fashion designer woke up naked and covered in a vast array of textures of color palettes. He blacked out again. His third fashion show was coming up and this had to be a home-run. The memories of critics' smug sneers sobered him. He grabbed the rusty scissors and his groupie's hair in his fist.

SUPER ICE

The ice cube dreamt of becoming a superhero ever since it was a drop of water. Everyone else wanted to chill, but he had loftier plans. Dress up in a fancy cape and tights and save the world. Kill the humans and set Mother Earth free. He lay in the ice tray dreaming, plotting, freezing...

THINK BIG

The cab driver was quiet until we pulled up to the restaurant and he saw my girl waiting for me. He turned around and revealed his yellow-toothed grin.

"You want some pills? Make your dick real big and you'll fuck all night."

"No thanks. I'm good, bruh."

"Give you good discount. No problem."

"I'm good."

BUSY

I got busy in a bathroom at Burger King. My girlfriend awkwardly bent over the toilet and held onto the rusted pipes for leverage. I wiped my greasy hands on her dress and hitched it over her peach-shaped ass. She bit her bottom lip as I entered her from behind and I went to work.

A MYTHICAL ENCOUNTER

Dexter spotted his father's liver-spotted head facedown in the grass. A unicorn hunched over the twitching body and neighed.

The unicorn removed its horn from his father's chest with a sickening pop, and Dexter slumped to his knees—sobbing. The unicorn's eyes were closed, but when its third opened, Dexter lost control of his bladder.

BURY ME DEEP

My elderly wife followed my will and testament to the last letter. My emaciated body was curled inside a biodegradable capsule and buried twelve feet deep. As the years passed, the red pine's roots fed off my corpse and it grew tall, blotting out the sky completely and shrouding my consciousness in a deeper darkness.

STUNTIN' LIKE MY DADDY

My left hand nervously played with Buddha hanging from the rearview mirror while my right gripped the stick shift. Flying Lotus blasted from the speakers. Reminded me of outer space. Wide open black expanses with glittering lights. A gunshot popped off. I stomped the clutch and shifted into fifth gear, blasting off into the void.

METH MOUTH

My teeth were going to hell. They kept me up at night. Constant grinding. Loss of enamel. Pale mushy gums. It was the drugs. Had to be. Grabbed my rusty 9mm and forced a jeweler to make me a gold grill. I inserted the fronts and shined for the first time in my miserable life.

BREAD & CIRCUSES

"The masses are in a frenzy. Not sure if they're buying the bullshit we feed them. What should we do?"

"Give them a new drug and tell the media to crack down on all fronts. Crank up the fear and get one of those MK Ultra bitches to twerk her ass."

"Sir, you are brilliant."

STITCH ME UP GENTLY

It took me two hours to sew the rottweiler's mouth shut. Bitch wouldn't stop snapping at my hands. Even now I can hear her whining and, underneath that, the voices. Spilling my secrets, yapping infidelities, dirty thoughts. Killing the thing wasn't an option. Stitches had to help, but they're slowly unraveling along with my ego.

ENLIGHTEN ME

Clusters of grey rocks spiraled into the cracked sky. Mossy green grass bubbled under my sneakers. I climbed a steep hill. It seemed endless. There were rumors of a man who reached enlightenment. A monk or a crazy hippie. I had to pick his brain, but I found the vultures beat me to the punch.

LAMB EYES

Work was killing me, so I texted this chick for advice. Told me to give my boss the "lamb eyes." Maybe I'll get off early. I strolled into his office and handed him a brown paper bag.

"Fuck is this?"

He opened the bag and screamed bloody murder.

"You know I only like doe eyes!"

THAT GOOD OLE-FASHIONED MAGIC

Papa taught me how to hold and tote the magic. He was a wrinkled shaman with calloused hands and a soft voice. When I was young, he brought me to *la playa* and buried a fig shaped like mother along with her hairbrush. She crawled out her grave, dusted herself off, and cussed him out.

FIRST DATE

Come over. Don't forget the alcohol. Let us weep together and swig whiskey and look up water bears on the internet with horrified faces and trembling fingers. Typing well into the night, bloodshot eyes reflecting the computer screen. Then fall asleep in each others arms, dreaming of moss piglets floating in the vacuum of space.

STOMPED OUT

Roger came to and his face felt like it got stomped by a herd of elephants. He inspected the red track marks imprinted on his temple. Were those sole designs characteristic of Nike, Adidas or some generic brand he would never be caught dead wearing? He went to the fridge, grabbed a beer and shrugged.

BLACK CHANDELIERS

My boss invited me over to his mansion. Vaulted ceilings, mink rugs, rare books, antique statues, custom pieces of art, but the one thing that stood out the most were the black chandeliers. Impossible to look away from. Shadows shimmered and slid across the glass until my boss placed his cold hand on my shoulder.

SELFIE

Zoey tilted her head askew and arched her back like Greek architecture, stretching her arm out, and stared into the camera phone. Click. Duck face. Click. A little cleavage. Click. Close up of amethyst earrings. Click. She snapped another photo, and her atoms split into a rainbow of fractals that would make a mathematician blush.

COMPULSORY FIGURES

My hand squeezed hers as we drifted onto an island of rose petals. The ocean spray caressed my grizzled face before she fished out a razor and carved a figure eight into my heart. She prayed it would crack the ice inside and release my pent up love. Sadly, it soiled her hands in red.

AN EYE FOR COMPOSITION

Christina held the plate of chocolate strawberries on her lap and admired the composition. Her father's baritone voice rang in her head.

"You always had an eye for photography."

She threw the plate across the room and it shattered.

"Fuck you, pops."

She flipped a middle finger and a phantom pain bloomed underneath her eyepatch.

LEAN ON ME

Rob shook his cup, enjoying the sound of ice cubes hitting one another. They resembled floating icebergs. Taking a sip of lean, he enjoyed the sweet syrupy taste. Reminded him of pancakes. Reminded him of home. His veins became cold passageways and his thoughts loosened and he shivered as he felt the avalanche come down.

RUN AND LOVE THE OLD AND KNOW TOMORROW

Justin Grimbol

BRAND NEW

The old lady walked up to the handsome lifeguard.

"So many young round women," she said. "They think my body is an abomination. They will be lucky to look this good when they are my age."

She winked at the muscular lifeguard. Then she walked up to the ocean and got killed by a wave.

TIME GOES ON FOR A
REALLY LONG FUCKING TIME

I touched her butt and wished her a Merry Christmas.

Then I robbed a bank.

Then I was put in jail.

By the time I got out, her butt was gone. I blamed it on yoga. Yoga did this to my poor Vanessa.

I walked to the ocean and got myself killed by a wave.

SPORTS ILLUSTRATED

I cut open my boil. It was the size of a baseball. Expected something gross to come out. Like green slimy stuff. Instead, confetti shot out of it. This was even more unsettling. I went to see the doctor. He gave me a handjob then told me to go on home and take a nap.

GRIMBOLS GO ON AN ADVENTURE AND TAKE THEIR MARRIAGE WITH THEM

We got lost. It felt really good. It felt better than walking somewhere I knew. There was a farm and a large field of soybean plants. There were old signs pointing to old trails that didn't exist anymore. My curvy wife and I argued. Then stumbled around until we weren't lost anymore. We drove home.

HOW CHILDREN HAPPEN

I took a really long bubble bath and came out so pruny. I looked like an old man. I looked so old, I actually had children, grandchildren and great grandchildren. I spent my remaining years getting to know them all. I warned them about baths and what happens when you stay in them too long.

FAMILY REUNION

The pizza was hot and burned the roof of my mouth. I treated the wounds with large pitchers of diet soda. By the end of the night I had drunk so much diet soda I thought I was going to have an anxiety attack. My family and I played Monopoly. I lost. Got sad. Cried.

DOING IT WELL

He was covered in lube and looking shiny. He had a boner.

"Relax!" he yelled. "Everyone will be okay."

There were a bunch of women. He had sex with them in lots of positions.

He liked the way buttholes looked when he did it doggy style.

Sex went on for a little bit. Then stopped.

IT'S IMPORTANT TO TALK ABOUT THE PEOPLE WE USED TO BE

I stuck my fingers in her and pulled out a piece of chalk.

"When I was young," she said, "I had an affair with my home economics teacher."

I probed some more. Found nothing.

We fucked.

I came. Then shat out a super soaker.

"I used to be an assassin," I said.

"Obviously," she said.

REALLY SEXY GARDEN STUFF

He stuck his dick in the venus flytrap. It latched on. Sure, the small plant could only fit a small portion of the head in its mouth, but he still felt really, really good.

Then they heard the door slam. And hundreds of flies buzzing and crying.

"Shit," he said. "I'm super allergic to flies."

NINJA 4:
REVENGE OF NINJA

The ninja killed him with a fork.

"I guess this was always meant to be," he said. "I just wish I could've taken you to that new Indian food place. The food there's... really good."

He coughed up blood and died.

The ninja walked to the kitchen, made some ramen.

Then disappeared into the shadows.

DIETING GIVES YOU REALLY POWERFUL MUSCLES

"This restaurant has really good ketchup."

"I like mustard most of the time."

"That's cool."

"I'm going to order sushi, just to fuck with the waitress."

"You shouldn't do that."

"It's what I'm going to do."

"I wish I could stop you somehow."

"Where is the waitress?"

"Probably crying in the bathroom."

"You're probably right."

NERD PROBLEMS

"Baby, I need to stop humping you."

"But why? I'm getting all jizzy down there."

"But I'm losing so much weight. I'm going to end up all skinny. I'm going to look like a nerd."

"Don't say that."

"But it's the truth."

"Fine, you can stop. You can stop humping me. I don't like nerds."

WISCONSIN FARM STAND

I drive to the farm stand. It's run by an old couple. A really old couple.

They are both covered in flies. I wonder if they have trained these flies. Maybe they are pet flies.

The elderly couple sell me corn and tell me to eat it uncooked. It's sweeter that way, they tell me.

NATURE PANTS

I drink a bottle of Diet Pepsi. I think about wearing a coat made of bear fur and going on hikes and peeing with my pants and underwear around my ankles, feeling the cool air on my ass. I want to hear rivers and worry about the weather. I mean *really* worry about the weather.

THROW MOSH PITS INTO THE CLOUDLESS SKY INSTEAD OF LETTING IT BE SO BLUE

I hear a bird screeching. And I think, Is this a fucking bird song? 'Cause this bird song is so fucking metal.

My dog is nervous. Her tail is between her legs. I decide to retreat.

There is more screeching. But I am too old to really get into it and start headbanging and shit.

MEDICAL STUFF IS SO FUCKING COMPLICATED

I thought I had finished painting my house, then I realized that the paint I was using was just water and my house is allergic to water, so now it's growing these really big boils. I plan on cutting open these boils, draining them, then posting the videos on YouTube for the world to see.

CELEBRATION

She bought me cake for my birthday and cake for Valentine's Day, then even more cake for New Year's Eve. Then I exploded and she used my guts to bake another cake. Then she cried over me, using the tears as frosting. And I gosta be honest, it feels good to know that people cry.

FANCY LIVING

I played golf all day. I wore sexy short shorts. The sun was hot. I got sunburnt. I spent the night on a yacht. I drank pus out of a champagne glass. I ate a whale. That night, ten women made sweet love to my sleeping body. I woke up early, ready for more golf.

CLASSIC WITCH PARTY

The triplets had faces like witches, only they were pretty. I got horny listening to them laugh and eat cake. I think they were stoned. I don't know. They caught me staring, though, and they took my clothes off. I just let them do it. Everyone at the party laughed at me. It was beautiful.

LOVE IS COMPLICATED

Valentine's Day involved a lot of buttholes. I licked like seven. Which is a personal record. Then I went to work smelling like buttholes, but I don't think anybody noticed. This made me sad. I mean, I got really, really depressed and quit my job and then spent a bunch of days playing video games.

BFFs

"I have to go potty," one teenager said.

"Just go then, man," said his best friend.

"Right here, in your bed?"

"Why not? We're best friends, aren't we? Plus, my sheets are waterproof."

"They are?"

"I piss on them all the time."

"Should we do it standing up?"

"How else would you piss the bed?"

WHAT WE DO

"You have eyes like a whale."

"Is that supposed to be a good thing?"

"It's the best thing. It's the only thing. It's the origin of music. It's the origin of boners."

"I guess."

"Can we kiss now? I'm super bored."

"Okay."

"I'm going to use a lot of tongue, so get ready for it."

INVENTION CONVENTION

They played spin the bottle until all their lips were chapped and bleeding. Their parents tried to stop them. The children hissed at them. Screaming, the adults ran from the house. They came back later with torches. The kids kept playing spin the bottle even as they burned. And that's how the sun was invented.

HOW WE STOPPED
GLOBAL WARMING

She wished her breasts were still covered in stretch marks. She wished her husband still liked to pop her frequent blackheads. She wished the gas station still sold gas instead of ghosts. Ghosts made for great inexpensive fuel, though.

"Fill'er up!" she said.

She bent over. Thousands of ghost dicks whistled in the lonely night.

A STORY ABOUT A GREAT MAN

The surfer rode the wave while listening to his walkman. He loved waves. He loved music. He loved sunshine.

Then a tentacle shot out of the water and pulled his swim suit down.

Everyone on the beach could see his decently sized penis.

They laughed at him.

He quit surfing forever. Then invented the Internet.

FULL GROWN ADULTS

"I just wanted to become a normal adult that smoked weed every once in a while. Preferably with a woman."

"That could still happen."

"You don't get it. I eat peanut butter sandwiches for lunch."

"I still eat Gogurt."

"My wife thinks I fart in my sleep, but that's just the way my dreams smell."

HEARTS BEAT LIKE THIS

"Your wife looks super hot."

"I know. It's her butthole. It's the best butthole in town."

"It's very soupy."

"It's clam chowder-ish."

"I think it's more like French onion soup."

"Maybe your tongue's fucked up. Smoke more weed. It helps."

"Is that woman really your wife?"

"No. I'm really good at being lonely."

"Me too."

HIGHER LEARNING

"I'm going to teach you how to bathe."

"Well, I'm a full grown man but I think it's good to learn new things."

"Exactly."

"Can you also teach me how to blink? My eyes hurt."

"I can teach you many things."

"I already feel really educated."

"When I'm done with you, you'll smell like paper."

PHANTOM FUCKING

Ghost sex was really fun. But messy.

"Stop jizzing!" Larry kept yelling.

"I cant. I bring forth the splooge of eternity."

Larry got up and left the ghost filling his room with green jizz.

Then he took a shower.

As soon as he felt the hot water on his back, he missed his ghost's jizz.

ROOMS

"Listen, you can cuddle with me. Just put your pecker in-between my butt cheeks."

"Thanks. I'm very non-sexual but I get boners and the smell of a stranger's neck sweat helps me sleep."

"In the morning, we can get breakfast. I'll make pancakes."

"If you end up being a disappointing room-mate, I might kill myself."

7-11 IN SAG HARBOR

Ducks roam to the 7-11 at dawn. A stoned cashier feeds them microwavable breakfast sandwiches. He remembers a bad joke and laughs. He remembers an even worse joke and laughs some more. The ducks love his treats. The sky turns all sorts of flavors. There aren't many customers. It's cold. Everything feels crisp and strong.

GET MARRIED TO THE SOUND OF THE TRAFFIC IN THE DISTANCE

I fondle her pubes. My wife smiles and yawns. I touch the pussy, then butthole. I smell my fingers.

Our dog rests at our feet.

Our laptops are warm.

"Can you set your alarm for seven in the morning?" she asks.

"Stop being so pushy," I say.

She laughs at me. It's a loving thing.

BIG TASTEY

The cookie screamed at the sun.

The sun winced at the warrior cookie.

"BIG TASTEY DOES WHAT HE WANTS!" the cookie yelled.

He jumped into the milk and let the air out of his pores, got damp, and fell apart, then died.

This is how all strong men die. It's a truth. The only truth.

WORKING WITH OLD PEOPLE

"You're really big," the old lady said.

"I know."

"Oh, you like that, do you? Well, how 'bout this? I think you are a big dumbbell."

"Be nice."

"I will not."

"You want more soup?"

"Of course I do."

"Here."

"IT'S TOO HOT!"

"Sorry."

"It's too hot."

"We'll let it cool down."

"Soup's too hot."

MORE ABOUT OLD PEOPLE

"My name used to be Sally Claudet. Then I got married to Ron Maxwell. I became Sally Maxwell. But he died. That was many years ago."

"WHAT? I CAN'T HEAR YOU. WHERE ARE WE RIGHT NOW?"

"I guess my name is Claudet again. Well, if I want it to be. My husband is very dead."

WINTER IN WISCONSIN

Teenagers ride their dirt bikes over the frozen river. I wait for them to pass. Then walk out onto the river with my dog and wife. It's a shallow section of the river. Maybe a foot or two deep. It's frozen straight through to the bottom. But I still worry about falling through the ice.

FUTURE GIZMO

My cell phone is filled with dick pics. I want to send them to everyone I know. I'm an adult, though. So I hold back.

Eventually I'll snap. I will send them to you. I will send you a picture of my balls so epic it will make you feel like the sky is falling.

SLEDDING

A new god snorted all the snow up his nose. It had been a long, cold winter and this new god got a vicious brain freeze. We stared up at the sky and watched him wince and moan and suffer. This is how the stars got invented. This is not how the darkness got invented.

DON'T TRY TO ESCAPE

I wanted to look rich so I taped a bunch of quarters to my body.

Then I walked around until I met some ladies.

"Nice outfit," they said.

I ran and they chased me. And we felt young. We felt like we had escaped something.

Then we all made out until our lips were chapped.

SCRATCH AND SNIFF EVERYTHING

I went around town sniffing butts. I made some friends. These friends were sexual. We got it on a little. But I had more butts to sniff. So I kept sniffing. I sniffed my way around the country. And kept sniffing. Sometimes I sniffed butts I was very allergic to, and I started crying uncontrollably.

DR. DAD

The doctor smelled like he hadn't showered in years. His nurse had an umbilical cord dangling from her teeth.

My parents had already given me a physical, so I couldn't even tell why I was there. I guess they just needed to make it seem official.

The doctor said my boner was thick and sniffable.

WHAT THE 90s WAS LIKE

My buddy and I watched horror movies and sucked on each other's dicks, then we walked into town and got giant sodas from the 7-11, hid out under the bridge and showed our buttholes to the boats that passed by, then we went to the video store and got more horror movies, and walked home.

HEAVY PETTING

That awkward moment when you realize you have been humping your own leg this entire time, and dogs just look at you like you are some kind of weird sex offender. You shake your leg at them, hoping they might give you some action, but they just walk the other direction. Leaving you lonely forever.

BODY PARTS

She had really big balls under her vagina. I licked them and her vagina dripped foaming body fluids onto me. She might have farted. It was hard to tell. Her balls got bigger. They smelled like pancakes. They smelled like love. They smelled like I needed to wash the dishes every once in a while.

WHAT BEING A NERD WAS LIKE IN THE 90s

I sat on my couch all summer, playing *Final Fantasy III* on Super Nintendo, eating Starbursts. I gained weight. Then I went on a low carb diet and I lost the weight. But I had a silly looking haircut and girls wouldn't make out with me. So I gained weight. Then I lost it again.

BATMAN

I walked into the cave and saw a giant bat with human breasts. The bat wanted to play Truth or Dare. I was into it.

"Truth or dare," she said.

"Dare."

"I dare you to pee on your own face."

"Nice move," I said. "I don't know what I was expecting, but it wasn't that."

THE CIRCLE OF LIFE

"Your butt crack smells like a tiger."

"Is that a bad thing?"

"I don't know. All I know is I'm really excited."

"What position should we do it in?"

"I only do missionary. You fucking love missionary."

"It's true. I love it all the time."

"Even during the day?"

"No, that would be fucked up."

RIP NIMOY

V'ger is heading back toward Earth. It heard of Spock's passing. It wants to get drunk with the other anomalies and maybe hook up a little. Then wake up all hungover and watch the movie *Angels In the Outfield* and start crying. Why *Angels In the Outfield*, you ask.

Why not *Angels In the Outfield*?

DUMPY PLACES ARE WHERE THE GOOSEBUMPS HIDE

Hugo sat at the other end of the bar sipping on a beer. It was just a cheap draft. Nothing fancy. Beer snobs would compare it to water. He liked that. It did taste a bit like a river to him. And people need rivers to forgive them. So he drank his beer very slowly.

WISHMASTER 5

I also wanted to see every butt crack spread open.

One time I met a Wishmaster. He told me he would grant me a wish. I told him about how I wanted to see all the butts. He got so bored he fell asleep. Then his boss fired him for not granting me my wish.

MARRIED IN RACINE, WISCONSIN

Sometimes I watch videos of nerds reviewing things instead of having sex with my wife and I think that life is pretty lame in a way that is seductive, then I force myself to get into some heavy fuckery and we bone until we are both tired. Then we watch some sitcoms on my laptop.

SPACE SHIPS LOOK BORING

I don't want to go into outer space anymore. I used to. I used to want to live in a world like the one in *Star Trek*. Now I just want to feel lonely in the woods and do it with hippy women, the kind that smell bad and laugh until their voices sound scratchy.

BRUSH YOUR TEETH

I pulled a tooth out of my mouth, sniffed it. It smelled old and ruthless. My dog woke up and looked at me with tired eyes. She smelled my tooth. She tried to eat it. I hid it under my pillow. In the morning, I looked under my pillow and found a two dollar bill.

BLACK OUT CENTRAL

It was a bad night. I woke up covered in tattoos of people's names I had never met and never loved. This was my first tattoo and it covered me from head to toe. Who were these people? And why did I need to remember them? I scratched my skin till it dripped warm blood.

HOW BABIES WERE MADE IN THE 90s

He loved humping buildings. He would hump them and ejaculate into them. Often the buildings would get pregnant. People would wonder why a baby Grimbol was growing in their living room. Then the building they lived in would push him out and they realized they loved the baby Grimbol. They even sorta kinda missed him.

PHANTOM TRIGGER

Nathaniel Lambert

CHAPTER 1

Man remembers shouldering a rifle for Relative Sam. He remembers the recoil, and his fading senses can still feel the barrel harmonics. He vividly recalls molten flack falling from the heavens, turning sand and flesh to ornamental glass.

That was long ago, but as he wanders a new desert, his finger grips a phantom trigger.

CHAPTER 2

"Who am I?"

"Who the fuck are you?"

Ancient Man in the plastic sled never answered. Never.

Man assumed there wasn't enough energy left in that desiccated vessel to respond, so he continued to pull Ancient Man on a child's sled to a destination just over the next dune, or mountain, or canyon, or horizon.

55 WORDS OF FORESHADOWING
(in G Minor)

Man sang the same cadence for the 1×10^6 time.

> *My girl's a vegetable*
> *She lives in a hospital*
> *She has no arms and legs*
> *All she has is wooden pegs*
> *But I'd buy her anything*
> *To keep that girl alive, yeah*

And then Man saw smoke rising up ahead. Real smoke. Not a mirage again.

CHAPTER 4

"My God. They're burning diesel fuel. I'd bet my shitty life on it."

(Ancient Man: ...)

"Do you think they have whiskey? My experience has been where there is fire and people, there is always whiskey. I've never been so thirsty in all my life."

Man trudged on, while the corpse of a metropolis rose ahead.

SCENE 5: TAKE 55

FADE IN

THE RUINS OF A ONCE GREAT CITY

Camera focuses in on our anti-hero pulling a red plastic sled down a decrepit street. The sled is packed with blankets, utensils, and what appears to be a lifeless body.

Piano music is heard in the distance.

MAN redirects his route, like a moth to flame.

CHAPTER 6

Man stood before the threshold of a post-apocalyptic-neowestern-diesel-driven watering and fucking hole.

"There are women and whiskey through those swinging doors, Ancient Man. Whiskey and women."

A crumpled wasp wing moan escaped from the sled.

(*Thirsty.*)

"I bet you could use a drink too, old friend. It will help us remember. I'm sure of it."

CHAPTER 7

The sled was tied to a hitching post outside THE POLE BARN. Man had promised his traveling companion a hand-delivered vessel of libation, but that was a lie. They both knew there were only enough coins for one... last... drink.

(Don't let me die here alone. Give me a damn pistol and someone to shoot.)

CHAPTER 8

There was a rickety stage to the left, buckling under the weight of flesh for sale.

To the right was a filthy bar top lined with shot glasses filled with a concoction that could be used to clean latrines. Patrons drank in assembly line fashion while ogling the goods.

Good thing Man was a multitasker.

CHAPTER 9

Man paid the bartender.

"I'm going to drink until I shit my pants."

"Wouldn't be the first time."

(*We're here for a reason. Remember?*)

Was it love? Revenge? He was convinced the memory lay at the bottom of one of the glasses.

The tricky part was staying vertical long enough to figure out which one.

CHAPTER 10

GENTLEMEN AND GENTLEMEN. PLEASE WELCOME COCO TO CENTER STAGE! SHE'S A NUBIAN PHOENIX RISING FROM THE ASHES OF THIS SCORCHED LAND! FEAST YOUR EYES UPON HER GLISTENING, EBONY FLESH! SHE WILL MESMERIZE, HYPNOTIZE, FANTASIZE AND IMMORTALIZE!

Is this/she why I crossed the desert? Man thought.

(*You dragged me all this way for a whore!*)

SCENE 11 TAKE 55_555

FADE IN

A DARK LIVING ROOM

MAN and LITTLE GIRL (father and daughter?) are huddled together. He wraps one arm around her shoulders. The other cradles a shotgun. There is a loud bang at the door.

MUFFLED VOICE: I want the girl! She wants her daughter!

MAN: Fuck you, you fuck! Over my dead body!

CHAPTER 12

Her eyes were long dead, but—*GAWD*—did her body thrive.

She wrapped around that pole and squeezed.

Fecundity. Her sex was vampiric, and Man wanted his life sucked right out of him.

An old scar streaked across her belly; ugly white against beautiful black.

That gash symbolized life beginning and, most likely, the end.

CHAPTER 13

Man traced that scar with his fingers in the air. He pretended to bury his face between those gorgeous tits. The desert had shriveled his balls to raisins, but when the blood got pumping, the pain was unbearable.

The whiskey kicked in. If he stood up from the bar now, he'd fall right into her.

CHAPTER 14 IS A FLASHBACK

"Daddy, will you make snow angels with me?"

"That's not snow, love."

"But it's fluffy and falls from the sky just like snow."

"It's nothing like snow, love. Remember, it will burn if we breathe it in. We have to stay inside now."

"Momma would make snow angels with me. If she was still here."

CHAPTER 15

Too in lust to notice the fella seated next to him with a face that had been repeatedly skull-fucked by a rhinoceros. This guy didn't appear to appreciate Man's amorous behavior toward the lovely Coco.

Man felt a sharp jab in his ribs.

"You're making eye fuck with my woman. For this, you must die."

CHAPTER 16

The desert heat cooked his reflexes. The hooch flagged his quicksilver speed. He traded his pistols and boiled the holster for soup. Whatever the excuse, Man never saw it coming.

A bottle upside the head and Tower of Man collapsed.

At least he could still see her.

Coco danced on as boot heels found flesh.

CHAPTER 17

"Take him outside, boys. We're going to have ourselves a helluva bonfire!"

Man could only see out of one eye. The other one was smeared like marmalade across the barroom floor.

What a waste of precious diesel, he thought as they strung him up.

The piano man played on as a match ignited human tinder.

CHAPTER 18

At the peak of the inferno, he almost— almost—remembered. He was there to find someone. But then it quickly faded, and all he could think of was the burn. It wasn't much different than the desert, just more in your face.

When the flames died, they took turns emptying their bladders on his remains.

CHAPTER 19

When you've been almost dead for so long, it takes a potent catalyst to finish the job (just ask Ancient Man). Man could probably thank/curse the desert for still being alive. It had cured him like jerky.

Someone squeezed his shoulder, while other hands lifted him in the air.

"Take him to see Mechanic."

CHAPTER 20

Man could still see through a slit of an eye. The whores were trying to save his life. There were so many of them. If his cock hadn't been disintegrated in the flames, he'd be tempted to use it.

They placed him gently on top of Ancient Man and pulled the sled down the road.

CHAPTER 21

The Mechanic woke from a fitful sleep, where nightmare images of meat and steel coalesced into breathing, fucking, and killing machines. A loud bang at the door meant another project had arrived.

He pressed a button on a swinging box. Bay doors riveted up loudly.

Coco brought the sled inside and they got to work.

CHAPTER 22

"It's too bad this time... I can't help you," Mechanic said while digging the head of an old screwdriver into a blister until it popped. "No way. What am I supposed to do with this? I'm not a miracle worker."

"But there are two of them. Isn't there enough between the two to save one?"

CHAPTER 23

Mechanic assessed what he had to work with. One was spent charcoal. The other was mummified. But he could feel life emanating—however weak—from them.

As Mechanic sketched out the flesh, metal, and silicone blueprints in his mind, he asked, "Why are they still alive?"

"Because they have a job to do," replied Coco.

SCENE 24 TAKE 55

FADE IN

THE SAME DARK LIVING ROOM

A loud crash is heard as the front door buckles inward. Marauders fill the room. MAN fires blindly into the crowd.

There are too many.

MARAUDER 1: You think a nuclear apocalypse could keep me away? All it did was clear out all the hiding places.

(MANIACAL LAUGHING)

CHAPTER 25

With his good arm, the one made of flesh, Mechanic licked his fingertips. He dug them into the wiring of his wheelchair while thumbing the ignition. Electricity traveled down his mechanized body and the wheelchair roared to life. He worked a throttle by his crotch.

He headed toward The Feeder. Coco followed with the sled.

CHAPTER 26

In simpler days, The Feeder had been some sort of farming equipment. Now, it was a welded mass of salvaged parts; an afterbirth of a long dead industrial abortion. It resembled a many-legged spider. Each appendage carried a different tool: drills, acetylene torches, circular saws, flashlights, wrenches.

Deep inside was a glow from life-giving embers.

CHAPTER 27

"Put them both on the table."

Mechanic reached behind the wheelchair, arm gyrating with the hum of hydraulics, and grabbed an extension cord protruding from The Feeder. In the middle of his chest was a rusted outlet. He plugged himself in. Or, he plugged The Feeder into himself.

He was ready to see his patients.

CHAPTER 28

The abomination of flesh, steel, and gasoline screamed to life. The galvanized arms tumbled and stretched until all of them balanced above Man and Ancient Man. This was a well-versed scene for the Mechanic. This warehouse, the chair, the floor-to-ceiling machinery grinding and pistoning away.

He began to whistle as he reached for the controls.

CHAPTER 29

"I'll use the head and neck of that one. The legs are shot, but I'll use strong rebar to reinforce."

Mechanic worked the controls. The Feeder plunged its appendages into flesh, stitching, cutting, replacing ruined biology with scrap metal and electronics.

"This project will need to be retrofitted with guns. Lots and lots of guns."

CHAPTER 30

The Feeder began to hitch, vibrate, and shake. Tired cursing. Thick black smoke billowed out of a rusted exhaust system. Gears seized and locked. Small flames belched out from electrical junctions. A long and sorrowful hiss escaped from deep within. Everything became deathly still. Mechanic did all he could for them.

"Do you approve, Coco?"

SCENE 31 TAKE 55

FADE IN

THE SAME DARK LIVINGROOM

MAN and LITTLE GIRL are surrounded by marauders.

MARAUDER 1: Give me the girl, and I'll let you live.

MAN: Fuck y—

MAN is bludgeoned from behind. He falls to the floor.

The camera switches to 1st POV of MAN. He sees them leave with the girl.

FADE OUT

CHAPTER 32

Coco admired Mechanic's handiwork.

Ancient Man's wrinkled face stitched with 12-gauge wiring to Man's torso.

Man's sinewy biceps welded to 1-stroke shoulder engines.

Pistoned knees. Motor oil and blood circulatory system. Central nervous system from a salvaged PC. Kevlar armor.

Gatling guns. Rocket propelled grenades. Lightweight, magazine-fed, gas-operated, air-cooled, shoulder-fired weapons.

"It's your greatest creation."

CHAPTER 33

"It's time to stand up."

Man-Ancient Man stood up slowly, struggling to keep balance until the internal gyroscope kicked in. It attempted to breathe. A fiberglass diaphragm flexed, forcing pungent air into polyurethane lungs.

It tried to speak. Adding machine paper streamed from the oral cavity.

WHAT SHOULD WE DO?

– END TRANSMISSION

"Kill them all."

CHAPTER 34 IS ANOTHER FLASHBACK

Man woke on the floor of an unfamiliar living room. He couldn't remember how he got there. In fact, he couldn't remember anything.

I was protecting something. I think.

Man winced when he stood up. His head was really killing him. He went out the shattered front door, and started his long search for... something.

CHAPTER 35 IS ANOTHER FLASHBACK

"Hey there, whippersnapper. Where you headed? You look like you're on an adventure. I love adventures!"

"Across the desert, I think."

"Well, shit, I'm coming with you."

"No. You're too old. I can't take care of you."

"I can take care of myself, buddy. I have this sled. We can take turns pulling each other."

CHAPTER 36

Man-Ancient Man stepped through the bay doors and opened fire. Nothing would be left standing when the triggers finally went *click*. As a hurricane of brass ammunition tore through brick and flesh, Man-Ancient Man began to remember everything.

I'm here for my daughter, and I'm here for Coco.

YOU KNEW THAT ALL ALONG
– END TRANSMISSION

CHAPTER 37

It spun around on well-oiled ball bearings, aiming all of its arsenal at the bewildered Mechanic.

WHERE DID COCO GO?
– END TRANSMISSION

"I... I don't know."

The head clicked to the side as if contemplating the next move. The gatling gun spun its death wheel. All that was left of the Mechanic was a smear.

CHAPTER 38

(You didn't come all this way only to kill that woman. Besides, I didn't see no little girl.)

THAT LITTLE GIRL IS MY DAUGHTER, AND NOW I CAN PROTECT HER.

– END TRANSMISSION

A pimp stepped out from a dark alleyway office. A golden grin was met with a MK-II grenade in his greasy bowels.

Kaboom!

CHAPTER 39

The doors of THE POLE BARN crumbled like moldy crackers under Man-Ancient Man's barrage. Man-Ancient Man briefly stopped to allow patrons to finish their last shot, and then it unleashed the heavens. When the smoke finally cleared, all that was left was sizzling meat wearing men's clothing.

A fleshy mass twitched on the barroom floor.

CHAPTER 40

WHERE IS COCO!?
– END TRANSMISSION
A hydraulic grip squeezed around the filthy neck of the one who had lit Man on fire. Blood, bones, and shit bubbled up through his mouth. He pointed toward a door in the back.

(*This one must surely die!*)

The grip tightened until there was no flesh left to squeeze.

CHAPTER 41

The back room presented more of a challenge for the Man Machine. They were waiting for it. They hid behind an overturned card table with automatic weapons at the ready. When it barged in, a fury of molten lead made holes in what little skin was left.

It came too far to be stopped here.

CHAPTER 42

In the desert, there was only Man and Ancient Man. They went weeks, months, maybe years without seeing another soul. However, they rarely spoke. All their concentration was focused on placing one boot in front of the other.

Now that they occupied the same body and mind, Ancient Man would not shut the fuck up.

CHAPTER 43

(*Holy Christ! Did you see that fella's head? It bloomed red like a spring flower! Look at that fucker there. Get 'em! Behind us. Don't move so Goddamn slow! You got guns, use them for Christ's sake. Kill them!*)

Man ~~Ancient Man~~ contemplated turning the arsenal on itself.

NOT YET.

STILL WORK TO DO.

– END TRANSMISSION

CHAPTER 44

A well-placed incendiary grenade fused its fleshy adversaries to the floor, but it had taken damage during the volley. Its right leg unit began to seize, dragging a sidewinder trail of blood and motor oil through the gore.

It stopped at the far wall, engines idling in anticipation. There appeared to be no exit out.

CHAPTER 45

"State your purpose," the wall addressed Man-Ancient Man.

MURDER. MAYHEM. CHAOS.

– END TRANSMISSION

"Who is your intended target?"

COCO.

– END TRANSMISSION

"Access granted. Please proceed forward."

The wall folded in like an accordion, and our mechanized anti-hero stepped through slowly.

The next room housed something like The Feeder, but this one was made for destruction.

CHAPTER 46

The room was alive, and it began to breathe. An amalgamate of wire conduit, gears, drive belts, and galvanized piping stitched together with slick, organic fibers heaved in and out all around Man-Ancient Man. It clicked its head upward as a giant, living hole opened in the ceiling.

Then the room swallowed Man-Ancient Man whole.

SCENE 47 TAKE 55

FADE IN

A PICTURESQUE CITY PARK ON A PERFECT SUMMER DAY

MAN, WOMAN, and LITTLE GIRL are enjoying a picnic on a blanket. Kites are flying. Everyone is smiling.

There is a loud rumble from off in the distance. The family turns to watch an enormous mushroom cloud bloom.

It eventually blocks out the sun.

CHAPTER 48

An afterbirth of man and machine spilled out into a giant marbled room. Man-Ancient Man righted itself and assessed its surroundings.

The hall was empty save for a polished steel throne at the far end. Coco sat upon the throne and waved lackadaisically.

Man-Ancient Man steamed forward at full throttle, all guns at the ready.

CHAPTER 49

WHY ARE YOU DOING THIS? WHY DID YOU SAVE US?

– END TRANSMISSION

"Because I'm so fucking bored, and this is what all of us deserve."

WE'RE GOING TO KILL YOU.

– END TRANSMISSION

"Dears, I've been dead ever since the bomb dropped."

WHERE IS MY DAUGHTER?

– END TRANSMISSION

"She's right behind you. Say hello to daddy."

CHAPTER 50

Something emerged from behind Coco and the throne. It had pigtails and wore a flowered summer dress. From the waist up, it was Man's daughter. But the bottom had been modified to resemble an industrialized arachnid. Tiny, many-jointed legs scurried toward Man-Ancient Man. Its eyes began to glow a brilliant red.

HI DADDY!

– END TRANSMISSION

CHAPTER 51

Father and daughter were finally reunited. Little Girl Unit's eyes opened wide like the iris of a camera. An amplified beam from a solid state laser burned a hole through Man-Ancient Man's abdomen.

It emitted an electrified scream and swung the gatling gun wildly at its daughter. She crashed against the wall and lay still.

CHAPTER 52

Coco stepped down from her throne and met her husband with open arms. They embraced. She was ready to die.

Ancient Man buried his rotted teeth in her neck and began to chew.

All weapon systems were armed, but at the last minute Man~~-Ancient Man~~ was unable to finish her.

(*She is still my wife.*)

CHAPTER 53

Coco had one more creation to show off. She whistled. Her throne morphed. The polished steel slowly separated into hundreds of razor-sharp blades held up by telescopic arms. They extended behind Man-Ancient Man and sliced; arms, legs, guns, and engines fell to the floor.

She tore Ancient Man's head from her neck and punted it.

CHAPTER 54

Coco was disappointed that it was unable to finish her off. "You couldn't go through with it." She looked down at the torso of the creature when the chest cavity burst open, and the head of Coco's ex-husband propelled forward, a bomb clenched between his teeth.

She hugged the head lovingly as the bomb detonated.

CHAPTER 55

All the leftover body parts of Man, Ancient Man, and Coco went inside the red plastic sled and were pulled back to the workshop by a spider walking machine. It had pigtails and laser eyes.

Mechanic had taught Little Girl Unit everything about creating life with The Feeder.

TIME TO MAKE NEW PARENTS.

– END TRANSMISSION

CARRION BLUES SONGBOOK

Josh Myers

FORGET ABOUT IT

It's been said that when someone tells you to get over depression, you should explain to them that that's like telling someone to get over a broken limb.

So when someone told me to "cheer up and get over" depression, I got very close, leaned into their ear, and whispered, "Where are your babies sleeping?"

NIGHTTIME DAYS ARE
ALL WEEKLESS

"What happened to the jumpers?"
"I don't know."
"It's the right time of year for it."
"The signs are up. That should have done something."
"..."
"Signs can be useful things."
"Is this you covering your tracks, or just shifting the blame?"
"Actions will be taken."
"Do that, if you're not too busy stepping around puddles."

"Some wine?" Laura asked.

"Wine? Ha!"

Kate produced a beer, bit the cap off, and drank it. She spun Laura into her arms, looked into her eyes.

"I'm Katherine fuckin' Ravelli, baby. I'm not like other girls."

Laura swooned. Kate kissed her.

Well, that would've been nice.

Instead, Kate sat, squeaked, "Yes, please, thank you."

CHATTERTON GOTTERDAMMERUNG
(With Respect to Charlie Balfour)

Jimmy sat in his stroller, watching the world. Waves of humanity going through the motions, stuck in hated jobs, loveless relationships, embracing what trapped them, ignoring everything that could set them free.

It was clear. He leapt from the stroller into the street, into the path of a speeding truck, screaming, "IT'S ABSURD! IT'S ABSURD!"

RYE

In times of uncertainty, it's best to surround yourself with the better things. Odd creatures that provide some form of comfort. Not really knowing what the issue is, in the confusion of friendship, they don't let you down. And you'll be grateful by the time that uncertainty passes, to have had a companion like him.

KING OF ALL LICE
OF WOOD SHIP BUILDING

"Yesterday I forgot how to do things."
"Yeah?"
"Yeah."
"Yeah?"
"Just up and forgot. Think I was thinking about them too much."
"What kind of things are we talking about?"
"All of 'em. Just for a little while, anyway."
"Really?"
"Yeah. Looked too close at how it was all done and got confused and forgot."

Oxide Dog In:
UTOPIA SYNDROME

"Oxide Dog, with this device, we'll finally be able to understand you!"

"Bark bark!" said Oxide Dog.

Mac Scientist clipped the device to Oxide Dog's collar and activated it.

"Well...?"

"NOW YOU FUCKED UP," said Oxide Dog.

Mac Scientist looked at his colleagues.

"NOW YOU FUCKED UP," said Oxide Dog. "NOW YOU FUCKED UP."

"...Oh."

THE DRUNKEN LORD OF
EVERYTHING

It can be too much, and most days it is.

He tried pills, found they made him into someone he's not. Settled instead for a more enjoyable, immediate solution.

Stop for a drink, the pain goes away.

Glimpses of bliss in doses he controls.

Might hurt friends, might scar lives.

But he survives another day.

I'M A DIFFERENT MAN,
SO THEY SAY

Peter woke up running.

The desert stretched endlessly in every direction. He heard gunshots, glanced over his shoulder. A man was chasing him. An older looking man, covered in ash, with thinning silver hair and large eyes. A man waving a gun.

"Get the fuck back here, Weller! Give it up! You're a dead man!"

WHEN ALL IS SETTLED AND DONE
THERE'S JUST EMPATHY CHAINS

Got real good at lying to yourself over the years. Simple things, only adding to a confusion that's spreading through you like a cancer. Question everything. Never accept what's in front of you. You could believe anything, but not this.

Too cynical for yourself. Too cynical for her.

And down beneath the ground, waters meet.

ANOTHER SPINNING FUCKING RAINBOW

A man with a thick Geordie accent sat across from me and said:

"D'you know why we don't come here? Because I... I've got dreams made of anvils."

He shook his head, put his hands on the table.

"I haven't got a boat."

He took a drink, said:

"I mean, have you even *seen* Scunthorpe?"

THIS IS PHILADELPHIA

Smack smack smack.

Hitler was trying to paint.

Smack smack smack.

Octopope sat across from him, slapping the desk.

"Nerrrrrd," Octopope said.

Hitler grumbled under his breath.

SMACK SMACK SMACK.

"FUCKIN' NERRRRRD," Octopope yelled.

"Do you mind?" Hitler asked in English.

"Borrrrred," said Octopope. "Do something cool."

"Like what?" Hitler sighed.

"I've got an idea."

EVERYBODY LOVES YOU

Sitting at work, perched on the steps to the offices upstairs, I look like a stupid fat gargoyle with a book and no fashion sense.

Meanwhile, in distant places, "friends" are talking about stealing my flesh. Making plans to flay the sugar skull tattoo from my arm.

Because they can't get that from anyone else.

ON DEAD MICE

Dig faster and try not to look back. Memories are dangerous things. Better men have folded under lower pressure and crafted new regrets.

There are no curtains. There's no ending here.

That pain in your head has been there a long time. It's not going away.

Consider what you've done.

And keep them with you.

IT APPEARS THAT
THE PARTY IS OVER

At work I hit my elbow on a display. A book falls from the top and lands with a smack.

Mine.

I pick it up, feel it mocking me.

"Wouldn't fall if I sold. Why haven't I sold?"

"Because I'm a dick."

I put it back, knowing I'll do it again to punish its behavior.

YOUR SHOELACES ARE BLEEDING

"You can't be done already. You've barely started."

"I worked very hard, thanks."

"Come on, I meant nothing by it."

"Always undermining my achievements..."

"Call this an achievement!"

"There you go again! Can't say anything nice."

"Oh, alright. Very good, lad. I'm proud of you."

"Thanks, Leslie."

He looked at the skull, grinning behind sunglasses.

BRENT BONESAW AND THE INFINITE MADNESS

"So just a heart and banner saying 'Tracy'?"

"Yup."

"You got it."

Brent started tattooing. His face centimeters from the skin. His eyes totally white.

Hours later, he wiped the area clean and looked at his work:

"*Gold in the hands of professionals. Malicious drop of blood and a great household. Blood bones black.*"

Perfect.

RELENTLESS CONFLICTION

Work was dead and we were drinking.

Conversation turned to one's ex, and memories of her chest. Then the guys remembered I was there and apologized for "excluding" me.

I laughed, "Boobs are wonderful creatures. It's the rest I'm not much interested in."

They laughed.

Then stopped.

And looked down.

Because we weren't so different.

BEAUTIFULLY, BLISSFULLY UNSETTLED

Nine years old at the supermarket. Looking at magazines, like always. This time I saw something different. Lance Bass on the cover of *TV Guide*, some makeup around one eye. I felt something I didn't think I should. I heard at school that it wasn't right. Eleven years later, I finally understood that it was.

MAKE EYES PRETTY WEAR A CLEAN DRESS

Kate smiled politely and took a sip of wine.
Oh, FUCK.
Laura looked over at her.
"How do you like the wine?" she asked.
Kate swallowed, thinking, *IT'S POISON I'VE BEEN POISONED SHE'S AN ASSASSIN SHE MEANS TO KILL ME THIS IS IT THIS IS HOW IT ALL—*
"Very nice," she said with a smile.

JOHN OF VIOLENCE

On his way to the bridge, he can't escape. Alcohol and sedatives always kept them at bay. The people he's hurt. The friendships he's betrayed. The lives he's destroyed. The things he's done he can't remember. The things he's done he can't forget.

On the bridge now, climbing over the rail.

Payback is a bitch.

TERMINUS FORSAKEN

They say walks are good for you.

Help you to get centered. To relax.

You can burn off some anxiety and, heck, even a few calories.

Walks are good for you.

But I remember standing on the bridge, feeling the wind on my back, pushing forward and thinking:

I bet it's closer than you think.

Oxide Dog In:
PIN LEGS MAKE HIS TORSO LEAK

In a remote pit, Mac Scientist examines a clay tablet, while Oxide Dog gazes into the distance.

"It appears to be some form of ancient writing," says Mac Scientist.

"Bark bark!"

"I'm trying," says Mac Scientist. "I believe it says... 'YOU DIRTY MOTHERFUCKER'."

He looks up.

"Now what could that-"

Oxide Dog farts an explosion.

ON OBVIOUS IDENTITIES

Constant questioning. A vast state of confusion from which there is no escape.

Attempts at rationalization are misguided. Sudden realizations in moments of clarity, inevitably to be contradicted and made to fuel the flames.

Nothing is binary. There is a scale and your place is never secure for long.

Who do you think you are?

HUNDREDS OF THOUSANDS OF BRIDGES FRY

"It's how. It's always how. That's all they're ever asking."

"I don't follow."

"How isn't important. The question to ask is why."

"*Why* did Hell become Hell?"

"A valid concern."

"Surely the how is every bit as important."

"Everything needs a reason to be before it can be."

"So you're saying the question is wrong."

LET ALONE MY PLASTIC DOLL

Lil' Mac lowered the pasta-strainer onto his head and announced, "I am going to the moon."

"You can't go to the moon," said his brother.

"That's what they told Buzz Aldrin."

His brother noticed Lil' Mac's headgear.

"What happened to the pasta?"

"I have no need for pasta where I'm going."

"But that was dinner."

THE FROWNING FACE OF
A PAINFUL PANCAKE
(With Respect, Again, to Charlie Balfour)

A clown walked into the church. His shoes squeaked as he joined the line for communion.

When he reached the priest, he stuck out a hand, said, "Body of Christ!"

A honk filled the church and water from a flower on the clown's lapel squirted onto the priest.

The priest stared.

The clown didn't move.

SOBBING WITH A
HUMAN SORT OF WAIL

"All we ever do is die."

"Yeah, yeah. Cute."

"A valid concern. What's in it for me?"

"That's no valid concern."

"What's in it for them?"

"A term for being too contented."

"And why would they not be better alive?"

"Sure, we'd have to beat them."

"That's no concern of mine."

"No valid concern, surely."

THE BULLETS OF HATE
STRIKE DEADLY AND CLEAN

He sat at the bar, bloody knuckles wrapped around his drink.

On the TV, news anchors were still frantically reporting the catastrophic plane crash five days earlier, desperately grasping at any new details.

He looked up, saw the same footage they'd been playing 24/7.

He sipped his drink.

Sighed.

All in a day's work.

DEEP SCHEDULES MATTER

I woke up, hit the light.

Sitting next to my head was a skull with a red pompadour, a neatly trimmed red beard, and sunglasses.

Before I could speak, it yelled in a gruff Northern English accent:

"Get the fuck outta bed, lad! No time to lose!"

And that's how I fought the Punk Wars.

SUZANNAH'S STILL ALIVE

The shed is cold. Everyone wants to leave. Been here two-and-a-half days. Three days, maybe. Don't even know what time it is.

Should be playing music, probably. There are instruments. Nobody cares.

"What's great," says the man with the guitar, "is he never even attempted."

"Fishes swim," says the girl with the saxophone, "like sperm."

Oxide Dog In:
OXIDE COP DOG BARK BARK
(For Joseph Bouthiette Jr.)

"We're in the clear!" said Jeff.

"We got so much!" said Billy-Jim-Todd. "There's like fifteen bucks here!"

"Ha ha!" said Jeff. "Crime!"

"Bark bark!"

"Oh no!" said Billy-Jim-Todd, turning around. "Oxide Dog!"

Oxide Dog stood behind them wearing a tiny policeman's hat.

"He's the police now!" said Billy-Jim-Todd.

"We're fucked!" said Jeff.

Oxide Dog sneezed.

VENGEANCE AS FONDANT

Some nights at work, when the shop is empty and town is dead, we get bored.

Sometimes when we get bored, we drink.

Sometimes when we drink, we open up about those who have wronged us.

And sometimes we look up websites to anonymously mail five pounds of actual genuine bullshit to our enemies' homes.

ON DITZY SCENES

It's something I don't like revisiting. It can send me right back. Blink and I'm in that place, with those thoughts, knowing there's no way out and a long way down.

It was a distinct possibility.

There are some days when I can't shake the feeling that it still is.

I tried to warn you.

THE SATURDAY DOLDRUMS OF BRIAN RIMPLEDICK, SOCCER DAD
(With Respect to Buffy Hastings)

Brian carries his wife's purse. He follows her through the shop. She makes no attempt to corral their children. He tries a few times before giving up. Again.

"Oh look, honey, you like this," she says.

Like he's a child.

Like he's a pet.

One day, he thinks, *I'll find the guts to do it.*

TAKE NO GOAT SHIT

After reading the final draft of his novel, Caleb sat with a sigh and thought, "No one's captured the struggles of the straight white male trust-fund grad student as perfectly as this. Truly I am *THE* voice of my generation."

Minutes later, he took his gun from the drawer and put it in his mouth.

ADD ANIMAL INSTINCT HERE

This is not my noise.

This is vicious and wicked and brings with it vicious and wicked things.

Clouds of insects pour from smoking holes left in the earth. A swarm makes its way through the wreckage. Locusts buzz and click and rattle. They carry with them a voice, and it echoes over the mountain.

COLDEST DAY OF THE YEAR

I open my wallet and count the cash inside.

$55.

I look at the single $5 bill. Just like any other bill you'd come across.

Except for one thing.

Written on it in Sharpie:

BLOCK BUSTER 50

I read the words and a chill runs through me.

I don't understand.

I believe I am cursed.

BACKLIT

Careening through space. This is a mistake. View from the airlock. Time spent mocking planets and spitting at stars. Hear noises and voices in frustrated silence. Missed childhood. Missed adolescence. Repressed hatred. Unpressed buttons. Direction to be adjusted. Something screaming. Stop being weird or we'll call the police.

Tell Ground Control you're never coming back.

YOU'RE THE ONE, YOU'RE THE ONE, YEAH, I KNOW YOU'RE THE ONE, YOU'RE THE ONE (YEAH, I KNOW YOU'RE THE ONE)

"So, what do you do?"

"I fly planes. You?"

Enoch looked at his arms, the blood drying on his skin.

"I guess I shoot people in the face."

"Hm."

"Yeah."

Silence.

Organ shifted. "Look," he said, "is it inappropriate to ask for your number?"

"I just killed someone."

"...Oh."

"But sure, you can have it."

I WILL GIVE MYSELF TO THE WAR

All this time spent waiting for something to happen.

I could've told you it wasn't worth it. While you're sweating and struggling to make something you think is important, someone out there is pissing around and gathering acclaim. In a year's time, no one will remember.

Your work will be forgotten.

You will be forgotten.

Oxide Dog In:
DO THE LONELY SUFFER MORE OR LESS OR JUST THE SAME AT THE POINT OF DEATH?

The audience applauded. Mac Scientist approached the podium.

Oxide Dog presented the award.

"Bark bark!" said Oxide Dog.

"It's an honor," said Mac Scientist, looking at the award.

A misshapen gold star with a lower-case *there was an attempt* engraved.

Oxide Dog sighed.

The audience was silent.

Mac Scientist took his award and walked home.

TAKE THE MONEY TO THE SUN

Lil' Mac stepped into the cardboard box and sat down.

"This is it, Jeff," he said, "I am going to the Moon."

"Sure you are."

"My wish is coming true."

"You bet it is."

"I'm going to be a Spaceman."

"Uh-huh."

"Could you close the hatch for me please?"

"The hatch?"

"The flaps."

"Oh, sure."

ON RED SLURS

There are no ulterior motives.

There is no secret meaning.

There are no questions to be answered. No mysteries to be solved. No secrets to be kept.

Not one more mistake left to be made.

There is only a man who tried to be good, and failing that, chose to bring himself to an end.

AS THE COLD REGRET
OF A HISTORY DIES

Beer's getting warm.

Shouldn't have come here. Meeting up with old friends is never a good idea. He knows that. And he still agreed.

Because he's a sap.

How long's he been waiting now? How long was it last time?

Brings the beer to his lips and it tastes like fire.

Downs it. Pays. Leaves.

IN A PARALLEL INSTANT
AN INFANT CRIES

A man sits at a switchboard.

On the wall next to him is a fuse-box and a black symbol.

The man tries combinations on the switchboard, flipping breakers that correspond according to a system only he understands.

The man wears a suit which is charred. It smells like smoke and he is aware of this.

BLOODY KNEES

The skull sits in the bathtub.

"Too many fuckin' bubbles, man!"

It has a red pompadour, beard, sunglasses.

"Too many fuckin' bubbles! Said I wanted bubbles, not all this! Look at it! Too many fuckin' bubbles!"

He's called Leslie.

"How'm I supposed to know if I'm clean or not? I'm under bubbles!"

Leslie isn't pleased.

WATCHED AFTER BY ANGELS

Sometimes when I go through my messenger bag, I find things I forgot were there. Usually it's a couple dollars or the name of a band or movie someone recommended. Little surprises that lift my dumb spirits.

Except for the night I found a piece of paper with *DO IT* written in someone else's handwriting.

QUITE THE MAN ABOUT TOWN

The cardboard box spaceship passed a group of shooting stars, flying so close that Lil' Mac could hear what the stars were saying. Lots of scientists have wondered what shooting stars say when they're shooting, but Lil' Mac was the first to hear firsthand.

They said:

"AAAAAAAAHHHH!"

"AAAAAAAAAAAAAAAAAAAAAAAAAAAAAAHH HHHHHHH!"

"AAAAAHHHHHHHH!"

He made a note of this.

COOP

Tried it once and it didn't work. Someone couldn't say goodbye. Lack of communication.

Tried it again. Out of five, I found him.

The way home. The anxiety.

The panic.

What am I doing? Is this good for me? Is this good for him?

All worth it.

For my friend.

My pal.

My Special Agent.

ALL THE CLOCKS ARE BROKEN

Early morning. Light just coming through windows.

Enoch was curled on the couch reading when he heard the car. He set the book down, watched the door.

The door opened. Kate stepped inside and locked the door behind her. Said, "It's only me."

"I can see that," Enoch said. "Whose blood is it this time?"

CABINET

I'd never heard anything like it before. Now I may never hear anything like it again.

A little man and a big daisy, beaming down on all creation, celebrating happiness and joy.

Of all of the influences.

Of all of the geniuses.

Of all of the voices.

You were the greatest.

You *are* the greatest.

BRAND NEW ORIGINAL SIN

Five men tied to chairs around the table, mouths duct-taped.

Grey-haired man with a priest's collar and scar on his forehead takes a seat, lays a switchblade on the table.

"Okay, boys, this game's called 'Who's the Dead Man?'"

Spins the knife.

Takes out a crooked cigar, lights it.

"Who's the fuckin' dead man?"

ON POKING DOGS

The time of the good night's sleep has come and gone. He's staring into his hands. Into his desk. Into the wood. Beyond the grain.

There's a voice out there somewhere, lost in the heaviness and the noise.

Trying to communicate.

For god's sake, listen.

But you've made your bed. You will lie awake forever.

CARRION BLUE

Consider what you've done. Keep them with you.

Attempts at rationalization are misguided. Nothing is binary.

No way out. A long way down. A distinct possibility.

A man who tried to be good. Not one mistake left to be made.

But you've made your bed. You will lie awake forever.

Where is your baby sleeping?

PRELUDE

Amelia Gulbranson

ARRESTED SCISSORATION

One day burger, french fries, and soda came to have a visit. They all met at french fries' house. The french fries waited and waited until they finally got there.

Burger was still not there. French fries and soda looked everywhere for him.

They turned on the radio news. "BURGER HAS BEEN ARRESTED BY DOUGHNUTS."

BLACK NACHOS OF DEATH

There was a cat named Black. He listened to Black Sabbath all day. His owner kept telling him to eat his lunch, but he wouldn't do it.

Black was always a mean cat. He scratched the baby. He scratched the kids.

He became an outside cat. They made him a home, but he ran away.

POP

Pop the Pig, he ran away. His story begins far from here. He liked to do his thing. His thing was eating ham and traveling around the world.

No matter where he went, people called him a cannibal.

One time he got caught in the butcher shop. Quickly he started talking to save his life.

SEAL SHOT IN THE BUTT

Once upon a time a seal got shot in the shoulder. They named her Valentine because it happened on Valentine's Day. They gave her a heart-shaped bandage. She took off like a rocket when they let her free. They were so surprised she did that. Then the seal said, "I wanted to be a clown!"

THE THANKFUL BOOK

I'm thankful for my baby sister, because she can climb walls better than a spider. I am thankful for my mom: she feeds me artichokes. I'm thankful for my dad, who is a ninja. I'm thankful for all my grandmas, because they are identical clones. I'm thankful for my uncles and grandpas and aunties.

Goodnight.

55 WORDS
ABOUT THE AUTHORS
(EXCEPT GABINO,
WHOSE BIO IS 555 WORDS,
BECAUSE HE'S AN ASSHOLE)

Joseph Bouthiette Jr. is co-editor of Carrion Blue 555 and author of the upcoming disappointment *MISTAKES WERE MADE*. He lives in a small Massachusetts town with a tailless cat and not nearly enough attractive women. Please forgive him, he has no idea what the fuck he's doing, and never seems to shut the fuck up.

Jess Gulbranson made a deal with his daughter: if, when she is older, she wants to do something he disapproves of, like joining the military or a cult, she must defeat him in single combat. He is the author of *Antipaladin Blues, 10 A BOOT STOMPING*, and should start practicing if he wants to survive.

William Pauley III is a guy that seems to stumble into your life, regardless of being welcomed or not. I once watched him eat 3,000 tacos inside his car—the wrapping paper almost made me suffocate. I knew he was doing it on purpose, just to see me squirm. Realized later it was a dream.

Gabino Iglesias was born somewhere, but then he moved to a different place. It's a long story, but he somehow ended up in Texas, where he has been learning to deal with the heat and the cold and the assholes and the hipsters that invade Austin every damn time there's one of those cool music festivals in town. The hipsters are probably the worst part of it, and he dreams of a day when killing them will not be punishable by law. He has worked as dog whisperer, witty communications professor, construction worker, hired muscle, and ballerina assassin. That last one is not a joke, and there are a few spots where bodies are buried. If you get him drunk enough and swear you will never tell a soul, chances are he will take you to one of these places and show you some bones. Be ready, because that's some spooky shit. But moving on, Iglesias now hides near a dumpster because he can't afford rent and works as a freelance journalist while impersonating a PhD student. His nonfiction has appeared in rags like *The New York Times*, *El Nuevo Día* and *Z Magazine*. The stuff that's made up has been published in places like *Bizarro Central*, *Paragraph Line*, *Divergent Magazine*, *Verbicide*, *Red Fez*, and a few pretty awesome horror and bizarro anthologies. When not writing or fighting ninja squirrels, he devours books and regurgitates reviews that are published in places like *Verbicide*, *Electric Literature*, *HorrorTalk*, *The Magazine of Bizarro Fiction*, *That Lit Site*, *Sundog Lit*, *Atticus Review*, *Heavy Feather Review*, *The Lazy Fascist Review*, *Buzzy Mag*, *Entropy*, and a few other print and online venues. He always has a hard time remembering all the names of the places he writes for and then feels fucking awful when he realizes he left out a few really cool ones that deserved to be mentioned. He really, really, really wishes he could get paid ridiculous sums of money for writing reviews, but that will probably never happen, despite the fact that he has tried to murder Michiko Kakutani on two separate occasions. In any case, Iglesias enjoys long walks on the beach (something that never fails to remind him of better days spent drinking at the beach with friends, some of them in bikinis), beer and cider, punching people who deserve it in the face, arm wrestling, remembering the 80s, and hanging out with his friends Oh, and buying books. The getting paid for reviews things? Yeah, that money would totally go toward purchasing books. And tacos. Lots and lots of tacos. Anyhoo, Iglesias is still surprised his first book was published and he tells himself there are more crazy editors and presses out there, so he keeps at it despite knowing that he has no real talent for it and having full knowledge of the fact that he will never make a damn cent doing it. The current bio started as a joke, but it eventually turned into a serious project that required seven hours of work, five drafts, three donuts, and calling Joseph Bouthiette Jr. a fucking asshole seventeen times. Iglesias would like to give a shout out to Josh Myers and William Pauley III for being cool dudes. Iglesias is currently working on overcoming his crippling hippopotomonstrosesquipedaliophobia. This is definitely not his first book.

Aleathia Drehmer only writes fiction when prodded these days. She maintains a somewhat daily blog called The Forked Road. She was once an editor of many things, but now spends her free time sewing, stitching, cooking, and walking her whiny Huskey. She makes her home in beautiful upstate New York. Catch up with Aleathia: http://theforkedroad-ajourney.blogspot.com/

Matthew Revert is a writer, musician and designer from Melbourne, Australia.
Matthew Revert is a writer, musician and designer from Melbourne, Australia.
Matthew Revert is a writer, musician and designer from Melbourne, Australia.
Matthew Revert is a writer, musician and designer from Melbourne, Australia.
Matthew Revert is a writer, musician and designer from Melbourne, Australia.

Grant Wamack is the author of *A Lightbulb's Lament* and *Notes From the Guts of a Hippo*. He is a weird fiction writer, Navy journalist, rapper extraordinaire, and urban mystic. You can find him dancing bachata with beautiful ghosts in the cobblestone streets of Southern Spain or you can peep his online presence here: http://grantwamack.com/

Justin Grimbol was raised by two husky ministers.

He went to college for a while. Then stopped.

Certain hymns make him cry.

His wife and he bought a dog. They cuddle on couches and make howling sounds together.

Grimbol books: *Naked Friends*, *The Creek*, *Hard Bodies*, *Drinking Until Morning*, *The Party Lords*, *The Crud Masters*.

55 words of adapted verse.

And you can hear it in **Nathaniel Lambert**'s accent when he talks.

See him walking down Fifth Avenue.

He's a Minnesotan in New York.

He's an alien. He's a legal alien.

He's a Minnesotan in New York.

He's an alien. He's a legal alien.

He's a Minnesotan in New York.

Josh Myers lives in Lambertville, New Jersey with his dog, FBI Special Agent Dale Cooper. He works at Farley's Bookshop in New Hope, PA. He reads and writes and sleeps quite a bit. His last book was *GUNS*. These things are supposed to be 55 words, but he isn't really 55 words worth of interesting.

This volume of 555 is **Amelia Gulbranson**'s first publication with Carrion Blue, and her second overall. She is six years old. Amelia enjoys writing, art, David Bowie, and monkey bars. Her favorite foods are fettuccine alfredo, hot cocoa, and broccoli. She is going to kick her dad's ass when the time comes. Don't tell him.

CATALOGUE BLUE 555

www.ingramcontent.com/pod-product-compliance
Lightning Source LLC
Chambersburg PA
CBHW031020120726
47905CB00007B/1988